Ramón del *Va*

Autumn & Winter Sonatas

The Memoirs of the Marquis of Bradomín

Translated from the Spanish and with an
Afterword by Margaret Jull Costa

Dedalus

Funded by
THE
ARTS
COUNCIL
OF ENGLAND

Dedalus made every effort to contact the rights' holders, without success, and would like to hear from them.

Published in the UK by Dedalus Ltd, Langford Lodge, St Judith's Lane, Sawtry, Cambs, PE17 5XE

ISBN 1 873982 83 6

Distributed in the USA by Subterranean, P.O. Box 160, 265 South 5th Street, Monroe, Oregon 97456

Distributed in Australia & New Zealand by Peribo Pty Ltd, 58 Beaumont Road, Mount Kuring-gai, NSW 2080

Distributed in Canada by Marginal Distribution, Unit 102, 277 George Street North, Peterborough, Ontario, KJ9 3G9

First published in Spain in 1902 (*Autumn Sonata*) and 1905 (*Winter Sonata*)
First published by Dedalus in 1998

Typeset by RefineCatch Limited, Bungay, Suffolk
Printed in Finland by WSOY

The translator would like to thank Ben Sherriff, Annella McDermot, Antonio Martin and Isabel del Río for all their help and advice.

THE TRANSLATOR

Margaret Jull Costa has translated many novels and short stories by Portuguese, Spanish and Latin American writers, amongst them Bernardo Atxaga, Mário de Sá-Carneiro, Arturo Pérez-Reverte, Carmen Martín Gaite, Juan José Saer and Luisa Valenzuela.

She was joint-winner of the Portuguese Translation Prize in 1992 for her translation of *The Book of Disquiet* by Fernando Pessoa and was shortlisted for the 1996 Prize for her translation of *The Relic* by Eça de Queiroz. With Javier Marías, she won the 1997 International IMPAC Dublin Literary Award for *A Heart So White*.

AUTUMN SONATA

'My adored love, I am dying and want only to see you.' Ah, I have long since lost that letter from poor Concha. It was full of a yearning sadness, redolent of violets and old love. I read no further, I merely kissed it. She had not written to me for nearly two years and there she was entreating me, painfully, ardently, to hurry to her side. The three sheets of paper, each headed by a coat of arms, bore the traces of her tears, and bore them for a long time after. Poor Concha was dying in the seclusion of the old Palacio de Brandeso and was calling to me, sighing. Those pale, fragrant, ideal hands that I had loved so much, were writing to me as they had in other times. I felt my eyes filling with tears. I had always hoped for a resurrection of our love. It was a hesitant, nostalgic hope that filled my life with the perfume of faith. It was the chimera of the future, the same sweet chimera that lies sleeping in the depths of blue lakes in which the stars of destiny are reflected. Ours was such a sad destiny! The old rose tree of our love was about to bloom again only to drop its petals piously on a tomb.

Poor Concha was dying!

I received her letter while I was in Viana del Prior where I went hunting every autumn. The Palacio de Brandeso is only a few leagues away. Before setting out, I wanted to hear what Concha's sisters, María Isabel and María Fernanda had to say, and so I went to see them. They were both nuns in a convent founded by one of the military orders. They came into the parlour and offered me their hands, the pure, noble hands of virgin brides. They both confirmed to me with a sigh that poor Concha was indeed dying. They both addressed me as 'tú' as they had when we were children. How often we had played together in the vast rooms of the old Palace!

I left the convent with my soul full of sadness. The bell was tolling, calling the nuns to communion. I went into the church and I knelt down in the shadow of a pillar. The church was still dark and empty. I could hear the footsteps of two ladies dressed in austere black who were visiting the altars. They looked like two sisters grieving for the same sorrow and pleading for the same grace. From time to time, they would murmur a few words and then, with a sigh, fall silent again. Thus, stiff and inconsolable, they visited each of the seven altars on either side of the church. The flickering, moribund flame from a lamp would alternately bathe them in its livid light, then plunge them into darkness. I heard them praying anxiously. In the pale hands of the woman in front, I could see a rosary. It was made of jet, and the cross and medallions of brilliant gold. I remembered that Concha had an identical rosary and remembered her unease whenever I used to play with it. Poor Concha was terribly devout and suffered because she believed our love affair was a mortal sin. Often, when I went into her boudoir at night, where she herself had arranged to meet me, I would find her on her knees, and I would sit down in an armchair and watch her praying. The rosary beads passed with pious slowness through her pale fingers. Sometimes, instead of waiting for her to finish, I would go over to her and surprise her. Then she would grow still paler and cover her eyes with her hands. I loved her sad mouth passionately, I loved those tight, tremulous lips, cold as the lips of a dead woman. Concha would nervously free herself from my embrace; she would get up and replace the rosary in her jewellery box. Then she would fling her arms about my neck, rest her head upon my shoulder, and she would weep out of a mixture of love and fear of eternal torment.

It was already dark by the time I got back from the convent. I spent the evening alone and sad, sitting in an armchair by the fire. I fell asleep and was awoken by loud knockings, which, in the silence of the early hours, sounded grave and terrifying. I jumped to my feet and opened the window. It was the same steward who had brought me Concha's letter and who had come to fetch me so that we could set out together.

The steward was an old man from the village and wore a hooded reed cloak and wooden clogs. He remained mounted on his mule by the door, holding another mule by the reins. In the darkness, I asked him:

'Is anything wrong, Brión?'

'It's nearly dawn, Señor Marqués.'

I hurried downstairs, not bothering to close the shutter that the wind was batting back and forth. We set off in all haste. When the steward had arrived, a few stars had still been shining in the sky. When we left, I could hear the cocks crowing in the village. We would still not get there much before nightfall, for the palace was nine leagues from there, along bridle-paths and across country. Brión went ahead to show me the way. We trotted through Quintana de San Clodio, besieged by the barking of dogs tethered beneath granaries, keeping guard on the threshing floors. By the time we got out into the open countryside, dawn was breaking. In the distance I saw some bare, sad hills, veiled in mist. Once we were past those, I saw more and still more. An ashen shroud of drizzle wrapped about them. They seemed never-ending, and the whole journey was the same. Far off, near La Puente del Prior, and despite the early hour, we saw a train of mules, and the mule driver, sitting sidesaddle on the nag bringing up the rear, was singing a Castilian song. The sun was just beginning to gild the tops of the mountains. Flocks of black-and-white sheep were scrambling up the slopes, and against the green backdrop of a meadow, we saw a huge covey of doves flying over the stately tower of a country mansion. Harried by the rain, we stopped at the old windmills in Gundar, and knocked boldly at the door as if that were our fiefdom. Two scrawny dogs appeared, which the steward shooed away; they were followed by a woman carrying a spindle. The steward greeted her in Christian fashion:

'Hail Mary most pure!'

And the woman replied:

'Conceived without sin!'

She was a poor, kindly soul. She saw that we were numb with cold, she saw our mules sheltering beneath the eaves, she saw the heavy sky with its dull threat of rain, and she humbly, hospitably ushered us in:

'Come in and sit by the fire. It's bad weather for travellers. This rain will flood the fields and they've only just been sown too. We've got a bad year ahead of us.'

We followed her in, but the steward immediately went outside again to get the saddlebags. I went over to the fireplace where a miserable fire was burning. The poor woman tried to get the fire going and brought in an armful of damp, green firewood that spat and gave off clouds of smoke. By an old door at the far end of the wall, the stone flagstones were white with flour; the door did not close properly and kept banging and banging. From behind the door came the sound of a mill working and the voice of an old man singing a song. The steward returned with the saddlebags slung over his shoulder.

'Here's our supper. My lady got up early to prepare it herself. With respect, sir, I think we should make the most of this break. If the rain sets in now, it won't clear up until nightfall.'

The woman approached us, solicitous and humble.

'I can put some trivets on the fire if you want to heat up your food.'

She did so and the steward began unpacking the saddlebags. He took out a great damask table cloth and spread it over the stone hearth. I, meanwhile, went and stood by the door. For a long time, I watched the grey curtain of undulating rain being buffeted by the wind. The steward came to me and said in a tone that was at once respectful and familiar:

'When you're ready, sir, you have a fine supper before you!'

I went back into the kitchen and sat down by the fire. I did not feel like eating and asked the steward simply to pour me a glass of wine. He obeyed in silence. He found the wineskin in the bottom of the saddlebags and poured some of the cheering red wine, grown in the palace's own vineyards, into one of those small silver goblets that our grandmothers had had made from Peruvian coins, one goblet per coin. I drank the wine down in one draught and, since the kitchen was still full of smoke, I went out again and stood by the door, telling the steward and the woman to continue their meal. The woman asked my leave to call in the old man who was singing in the other room. She shouted to him:

'Father! Father!'

He came in, all white with flour, his cap to one side, a song still on his lips. He was an old man with sparkling eyes and a shock of white hair, as cheerful and shrewd as a book of ancient proverbs. They drew up two rough, smoke-blackened footstools and, amidst a chorus of blessings, they sat down to eat round the hearth. The two scrawny dogs prowled about nearby. It was a banquet in which our every need had been catered for by poor, sick Concha. Those pale hands, which I so loved, were serving at the table of the humble like the anointed hands of saintly princesses! When he tasted the wine, the old man rose to his feet crying:

'Here's to the health of the good gentleman who has given us this wine. In years to come I hope to drink your health again in your noble presence.'

Then, equally ceremoniously, the woman and the steward drank too. While they were eating, I heard them talking in low voices. The man was asking where we were going and the steward told them that we were heading for the Palacio de Brandeso. The man knew the road, for he still paid an ancient levy to the lady of the palace — a levy of two sheep, three bushels of wheat and three of barley. The previous year, she had excused him the whole amount because the drought was so bad. She was a woman who took pity on the poor villagers. I listened from the door, watching the rain fall, and I felt touched and pleased. I turned and peered at them through the smoke. Then they lowered their voices still more and appeared to be talking about me. The steward got up.

'If you're ready sir, we could give some food to the mules and then set off again.'

He went out with the old man, who was eager to help. The woman started sweeping up the ashes from the hearth. At the back of the kitchen, the dogs were gnawing on a bone. While she swept, the poor woman kept up a stream of mumbled blessings, as if she were praying:

'May the Lord grant you all the good fortune and health in the world, and when you reach the palace may you be very happy. May you find the lady well and with roses in her cheeks.'

As she walked round and round the fireplace, the woman was monotonously intoning:

'May you find her like a rose on a rose bush!'

Taking advantage of a break in the rain, the steward came in to pick up the saddlebags from the kitchen while the old man untethered the mules and led them out to the road so that we could mount up. His daughter came to the door to watch us leave:

'God grant the noble gentleman every happiness! May the Lord go with you!'

When we had mounted, she came out onto the road, covering her head with her apron to keep off the rain, which had started up again; she approached me in mysterious fashion. She looked like some millenarian shade. She was trembling and her eyes burned feverishly beneath the hood formed by her apron. She was clutching a handful of herbs and she gave them to me with a sibylline look on her face, murmuring:

'When my lady the Countess is not looking, place these herbs beneath her pillow. They'll make her better. Souls are like nightingales, all they want is to fly away. The nightingales happily sing in gardens, but in the palaces of kings they slowly die.'

She raised her arms as if to evoke a distant, prophetic thought, then let them fall again. The old man came over, smiling, and drew his daughter away to the side of the road so that my mule could pass.

'Take no notice of her, sir. She's a bit simple.'

I felt superstition pass like a shadow over my soul, and I silently took that handful of rain-soaked herbs. Ah, those holy, scented herbs that serve equally well as a cure for heartsickness and as a cure for the ailments of sheep, as an aid to increasing family virtues and to swelling the harvest . . . It would not be long before they were blooming on Concha's grave in the green, sweet-smelling cemetery of San Clodio de Brandeso!

I had only a vague memory of the Palacio de Brandeso; I used to go there as a child with my mother. I remembered the old garden and the maze that had both frightened and attracted me. After many years, I was returning, answering the call of the same girl with whom I had so often played in the old flowerless garden. The setting sun touched with gold the sombre dark greens of the venerable trees – the cedars and cypresses that were as old as the palace itself. A stone archway led into the garden and, carved in the stone above the cornice, there were four shields bearing the coat of arms of four different lineages, those of the founder's grandparents, who had all been of noble birth. When we came in sight of the palace, our weary mules broke into a brisk trot and approached the door on which they then knocked with their hooves. A villager dressed in rough serge, who was waiting there, hurried over to hold my stirrup for me. I jumped down and handed him the reins. Brimming with memories, I walked down the dark, leaf-strewn avenue of chestnut trees. At the other end, I could see the palace with all its windows shut and the window panes lit by the sun. Suddenly, I saw a white shadow appear at one of the windows, I saw it stop and raise two hands to its forehead. Then the middle window slowly opened and the white shadow leaned out to greet me, waving its ghost-like arms. It was only a moment. The branches of the chestnut trees blocked my view and I could no longer see. When I emerged from the avenue of trees, I again looked up at the palace. All the windows were closed, including the one in the middle. With my heart pounding, I went into the great, dark, silent hallway. My footsteps echoed on the broad flagstones. Sitting on the oak stairs, worn smooth with use, there were people waiting to pay some levy or other. At the far end, I could make out the massive old chests for storing wheat, the lids raised. When the tenant farmers saw me come in, they got to their feet, mumbling respectfully:

'A very good evening to you, sir.'

Then they slowly sat down again, almost swallowed up in the shadow cast by the wall. I hurried up the magnificent staircase with its broad steps and roughly carved granite bannister. Before I reached the top, a door swung silently open and an ancient maidservant peered out; it was Concha's old nursemaid. Carrying a large candle in her hand, she came down the stairs to meet me:

'May God reward you for coming. My lady will see you now. She's spent so long just waiting for you to come, sir. She didn't want to write to you. She thought you would have forgotten her. I was the one who convinced her that you wouldn't have. You hadn't, had you, Marquis?'

I could only murmur:

'Of course not, but where is she?'

'She's been lying down all afternoon. She wanted to be in her best clothes when you arrived. She's like a child – well, you know what she's like. She got to the point where she was shaking with impatience and had to lie down.'

'Is she that ill?'

The old woman's eyes filled with tears:

'She's very ill, sir. You wouldn't recognise her.'

She passed her hand over her eyes and added in a low voice, pointing to the lit door at the other end of the corridor:

'She's in there.'

We walked on in silence. Concha heard my footsteps and called out in an anguished voice from the depths of the room:

'You're here, my love, you're here!'

I went in. Concha was sitting up, reclining against the pillows. She gave a cry and, instead of holding out her arms to me, covered her face with her hands and began to sob. The maidservant put the candle down on the bedside table and left, sighing. Trembling, touched by her reaction, I went over to Concha. I kissed the hands with which she was still covering her face and gently pulled them away. She gave me a long look, but did not speak; her eyes, the beautiful eyes of one mortally ill, were full of love. Then she half-closed them and fell back in a languid, happy swoon. I watched her for a moment. She was so pale! I felt an anxious knot in my throat. She slowly opened her eyes and, then, cupping my head in her burning hands, she looked at me again with a look that seemed imbued with the melancholy of love and with the death that was now closing in upon her.

'I was afraid you wouldn't come.'

'And now?'

'Now, I'm happy.'

Her mouth, a rose drained of colour, was trembling. Again she closed her eyes with pleasure, as if to store up in her memory a beloved vision. My heart contracted, for I realised she was dying.

Concha sat up to reach for the bell. I gently caught her hand:

'What do you want?'

'I want to call my maid so that she can come and help me dress.'

'Now?'

'Yes.'

She leaned her head back and added with a sad smile:

'I want to welcome you properly to the palace.'

I tried to persuade her not to get up. She insisted:

'I'm going to order them to lay a fire in the dining room, a good fire. You'll dine with me tonight.'

And her eyes, still wet with tears, in that palest of pale faces, were full of loving, happy sweetness.

'I wanted to be up when you came, but I just couldn't. I was dying of impatience and made myself ill.'

I still had her hand in mine, and I kissed it. We looked at each other, smiling.

'Why don't *you* call?'

I said in a low voice:

'Let me be your maid.'

Concha removed her hand from between mine.

'You do have some mad ideas!'

'Not that mad. Where are your clothes?'

Concha smiled like a mother at a small child's caprice.

'I don't know . . .'

'Come on, tell me.'

'I don't know, really I don't!'

At the same time, with a charming gesture of eyes and lips, she indicated a large oak wardrobe at the foot of the bed. The key was in the door and I opened it. The wardrobe exhaled a delicate, ancient fragrance. In it were the clothes that Concha had been wearing that day.

'Are these the clothes?'

'Yes, I just need that white dressing gown.'

'Won't you be cold?'

'No.'

I removed the gown from its hanger; it seemed still to exude a perfumed warmth and Concha murmured, blushing:

'You and your odd ideas . . .'

She swung her feet out of the bed, those white, childlike, almost fragile feet, in which blue veins traced paths made for kisses. She shivered slightly as she put on her sable slippers and said in an oddly gentle voice:

'Now open that long drawer and choose some silk stockings for me.'

I chose a pair in black silk, embroidered with little mauve arrows.

'These ones?'

'Yes, whichever ones you like.'

To put them on, I knelt down on the tiger skin by her bed. Concha protested:

'Get up! I don't want to see you like that.'

I smiled and paid no heed. Her feet struggled to flee my hands, poor feet that I could not help but kiss. Concha trembled and exclaimed delightedly:

'You don't change, do you?'

After putting the silk stockings on her, I slipped on her garters, which were also made of silk – two white ribbons with gold fastenings. I dressed her with the religious, loving care with which devout ladies dress the images they serve as handmaidens. When, with tremulous hands, I had tied the ribbons of that white robe, like a nun's habit, beneath her delicate, round, pale bust, Concha stood up, leaning on my shoulders for support. With the ghostly gait that some women acquire when they are very ill, she walked over to the dressing table and looked into the mirror to arrange her hair.

'How pale I am! I'm nothing but skin and bone.'

I said:

'I hadn't noticed, Concha.'

She smiled mirthlessly.

'Tell me honestly, how do I look?'

18

'Once you were the princess of the sun, and now you are the princess of the moon.'

'Liar!'

And she turned her back on the mirror to look at me. At the same time, she tapped a gong placed near the dressing table. Her old nursemaid came hurrying in.

'Did you call, my lady?'

'Yes, have the fire lit in the dining room.'

'We've already put a brazier in there.'

'Well, take it out again. Have them light the fire.'

The maid looked at me:

'Do you really want to go down to the dining room with my lady, bearing in mind how cold it is along these corridors?'

Concha went and sat shivering at one end of the sofa, carefully wrapping the ample dressing gown about her. She said:

'I'll put on a shawl to walk down the corridors.'

And turning to me – since I said nothing, not wishing to contradict her – she murmured lovingly and submissively:

'If you don't want me to, I won't.'

I said sadly:

'It's not that I don't want you to, Concha, I just don't want to harm you in any way.'

She sighed:

'I didn't want you to be on your own.'

Then, with the rough, kindly loyalty of old servants, Concha's former nursemaid said:

'It's only natural that you should want to be together, and that's why I thought you could eat at the table in here. What do you think, my lady? And you, Señor Marqués?'

Concha placed her hand on my shoulder, and replied, smiling:

'You're extremely clever, Candelaria. Both the Marquis and I are very impressed. Tell Teresina that we will eat in here.'

We were left alone again. Her eyes brimming with tears, Concha held out one hand to me and I kissed her fingers, as I used to do, making a pale rose bloom on each fingertip. There was a bright fire burning in the grate. Concha was sitting on the carpet, one elbow resting on my knees, and was stirring the logs with the bronze tongs. As the flames flickered and grew, they left a rosy glow on the eucharistic whiteness of her skin, like the sun on the ancient carved marble statues in Pharos.

She put down the tongs and held out her arms to me so that I could help her to her feet. We looked at each other; I could see myself reflected in her eyes, which shone with the happiness of a child bubbling with laughter after a now forgotten crying fit. The table was already laid with a cloth and so, still holding hands, we went over and sat on the chairs that Teresina had just drawn up. Concha said to me:

'Can you remember how long ago it is since you were here with your poor mother, Aunt Soledad?'

'Yes, can you?'

'Twenty-three years ago. I was eight. That was when I first fell in love with you. How I suffered watching you playing with my older sisters. It seems incredible that a child can suffer so from jealousy. I've shed more than enough tears over you as a grown woman too, but then I've had the consolation of being able to tell you off.'

'And yet you've always been so sure of my affection for you. Your letter makes that absolutely clear.'

Concha tried to blink back the tears trembling on her eyelashes.

'It wasn't your affection I was sure of, it was your compassion.'

She gave a melancholy smile, and two tears shone in her eyes. I made to get up and console her, but she stopped me with a gesture. Teresina came in. We started eating in silence. To hide her tears, Concha raised her glass and drank slowly; when she put the glass down on the table cloth, I took it from her hand and placed my lips where she had placed hers. Concha turned to her maid.

'Tell Candelaria to come and serve us.'

Teresina went out and we smiled at each other.

'Why did you ask for Candelaria to come?'

'Because I'm afraid of you, and, besides, nothing shocks poor Candelaria any more.'

'Candelaria is as indulgent towards our love as any good Jesuit might be.'

'Now don't let's start!' Concha shook her head in mock anger, at the same time placing a finger on her pale lips: 'I won't have you posing as an Aretino or as a Cesare Borgia.'

Poor Concha was very devout and the aesthetic admiration I had felt in my youth for the son of Alexander VI frightened her as much as if it were some cult of the Devil. With an exaggerated gesture that mingled good humour and genuine unease, she ordered me to be silent:

'Be quiet now!'

Looking at me out of the corner of her eye, she slowly turned her head:

'Candelaria, pour some wine into my glass.'

Candelaria was at that moment standing with her back to the chair, her hands folded over her starched, white pinafore; she hurried to serve her mistress. Concha's words, which seemed perfumed with happiness, faltered into a groan. I saw her close her eyes with a look of anguish, and her mouth, that pale, sickly rose, grew paler still. I got up, frightened.

'What's wrong? What's wrong?'

She couldn't speak. Her head fell back against the chair. Candelaria ran into the bedroom and brought some smelling salts. Concha gave a sigh and opened her eyes, staring about her, vague and lost, as if waking from a dream peopled with monsters. Fixing her gaze on me, she murmured weakly:

'It's nothing. It's just your fear I can feel.'

Then, drawing one hand across her forehead, she took a deep breath. I made her take a few sips of soup. She revived a little and, though still pale, managed a tenuous smile. She bade me sit down again and continued drinking the soup by herself. When she had finished, she picked up the glass of wine with delicate fingers and kindly, tremulously offered it to me. I took a sip to please her. Concha drank the rest and then drank nothing else all evening.

We were sitting on the sofa and had been talking for a long time. Poor Concha was telling me about her life during the two years in which we had not seen each other – one of those silent, resigned lives that watches the days pass with a sad smile and weeps at night in the darkness. I did not need to tell her about my life. Her eyes seemed to have been following it from afar and she knew everything. Poor Concha! Seeing her so ill and drawn, and so very different from the woman she had been, I felt a sharp pang of regret for having done as she had asked that night when she had knelt before me, weeping, and had begged me to go, to forget her. Her mother, a solemn, devout widow, had come to see us in order to put an end to our relationship. Neither of us wanted to remember the past, however, and we sat in silence, she resigned and I with a sombre, tragic look on my face – it makes me smile now to think of it. I had almost forgotten it, because women do not fall in love with old men, and it is a look that only suits young Don Juans. Were a young girl, a spiritual creature full of grace and candour, to fall in love with me with my white hair, my hollow cheeks, my august, senatorial beard, I would deem it criminal to adopt any other attitude with her than that of an old prelate – a confessor of princesses and a theologian of love. But that look, like a repentant Satan, excited poor Concha, made her tremble. She was so very, very good, which was why she was so very unhappy. A painful smile, like the soul of a languishing flower, flickered across her lips and she murmured:

'How different our lives might have been.'

'I know. I can't understand now why I did as you asked. I probably couldn't bear the sight of you crying.'

'Don't tell fibs. I felt sure you would come back. My mother was always terrified that you would.'

'I didn't come back because I was waiting for you to call me – that devilish pride of mine.'

'It wasn't pride, it was another woman. You'd been deceiving me with her for a long time. When I found out, I thought I would die. I was so desperate that I even agreed to go back to my husband.'

She folded her hands, looking at me intensely, her voice grown husky, her pale lips trembling. She said with a sob:

'You can't imagine how it hurt me when I guessed why you hadn't come, and yet I've never borne you a moment's malice.'

I did not dare deceive her then and, out of sentiment, I remained silent. Concha stroked my hair and, lacing her fingers together, placed her hands on my forehead. Sighing, she said:

'What a stormy time you've had of it these last two years. Your hair's almost white.'

I gave an equally pained sigh:

'Too many griefs, Concha.'

'No, that's not why you've gone white. There must be some other reason. Your griefs can never equal mine, and my hair isn't white.'

I sat up to look at her. She removed the gold pin holding her hair in place and which then fell to her shoulders like a black, silken wave.

'Now your forehead shines like a star beneath your parted ebony hair. You are white and pale as the moon. Do you remember when I used to ask you to whip me with your hair? Cover me with it now, Concha.'

Loving and indulgent, she spread the perfumed veil of her hair over me. I breathed it in, my face submerged in it as if in a holy fountain, and my soul filled with delight and bloomed with memories. Concha's heart was beating hard; with shaking hands I unlaced her robe and my lips kissed skin that was anointed with love as if with a balm.

'My love!'

'My love!'

Concha closed her eyes for a moment, then, getting to her feet, she gathered up her long hair.

'Please, for God's sake, go!'

24

I smiled at her.

'Where exactly do you want me to go?'

'Just go. All this emotion is killing me. I need to rest. I wrote asking you to come precisely because there can be nothing between us now but a kind of ideal affection. You must understand that, in my state of health, there couldn't possibly be anything more. It would be too terrible to die in mortal sin!'

Looking paler than ever, she folded her arms and rested her hands on her shoulders in a resigned, noble pose she often adopted. I moved towards the door.

'Goodnight then, Concha.'

She sighed.

'Goodnight.'

'Would you mind calling Candelaria to guide me along the corridors?'

'Ah, of course, you don't yet know the way.'

She went over to the dressing table and beat on the gong. We waited in silence, but no one came. Concha looked at me uncertainly.

'Candelaria's probably gone to bed.'

'In that case . . .'

She saw me smile and, looking sad and serious, she shook her head.

'In that case, I will guide you.'

'You mustn't catch cold.'

'I'm all right.'

She picked up one of the candlesticks from the dressing table and hurried out, dragging behind her the long train of her gown. At the door, she turned, calling to me with her eyes, then, white as a ghost, she disappeared into the darkness of the corridor. I followed and caught up with her.

'You're mad!'

She chuckled to herself and leaned upon my arm. At a point where two corridors met, we came upon a large, bare, round anteroom full of ancient chests and hung with pictures of saints. On one wall, a nightlight cast a pale circle about the livid, lacerated feet of Jesus. Then we saw the shadowy form of a woman huddled in one corner of the balcony window. She was sound asleep, her hands folded in her lap, her head on her chest. It was Candelaria, who woke, startled, at the sound of our footsteps.

'I was waiting to show you to your room, Marquis.'

Concha said:

'I thought you'd gone to bed.'

We continued in silence until we reached the half-open door of a room in which a light could be seen. Concha let go of my arm and stood there trembling and very pale. In the end she came in. This was my room. On an old console table stood a silver candelabra with the candles burning. At the far end I could see the bed hung with ancient damask curtains. Concha inspected everything with maternal care. She paused to smell the fresh roses in a vase and then said goodnight.

'I'll see you tomorrow.'

I picked her up in my arms as if she were a child.

'I won't let you go.'

'You must.'

'No, I won't.'

And my eyes smiled into her eyes, and my mouth smiled upon her mouth. Her Turkish slippers fell from her feet and I carried her over to the bed, where I lovingly lay her down. Then she happily submitted. Her eyes shone and two roses bloomed on the white skin of her cheeks. She gently removed my hands and, slightly embarrassed, began unlacing her white robe that slipped away from her pale, trembling body. I pulled back the sheets and she slid between them. She began to sob and I sat beside her, consoling her, until, at last, she appeared to fall asleep. Only then did I lie down too.

All night I felt the presence beside me of that poor body burning with fever, like a sepulchral light in an opaque white porcelain vase. Her head rested on the pillow, framed by a wave of black hair that emphasised the matt pallor of her face; her mouth, drained of colour, her hollow cheeks, her drawn forehead, her waxen eyelids, her eyes set in dark, hollow sockets, gave her the spiritual appearance of a lovely saint consumed by penitence and fasting. Her neck bloomed upon her shoulders like a sickly lily, her breasts were two white roses perfuming an altar, and her slender arms, delicate and fragile, were like the handles of an amphora circling her head. Leaning on the pillows, I watched over her exhausted, sweat-drenched sleep. The cockerel had crowed twice and the whitish light of dawn was seeping in through the closed balcony doors. On the ceiling, the shadows obeyed the flickering of the candles, which, having burned all night, were sputtering out in the silver candelabra. Near the bed, on an armchair, hung my hunter's cape, still damp from the rain, and sprinkled over it were those herbs whose secret properties were known only to the poor mad woman at the mill. I slid out of bed and gathered them up. With a strange blend of superstition and irony, taking care not to wake her, I concealed that mystical bunch of herbs beneath Concha's pillows. I lay down, placed my lips on her perfumed hair and gradually slipped into sleep. For a long time, the vision of that day floated in my dreams, with its faint taste of tears and smiles. I woke once, I believe, and saw Concha sitting by my side; I think she kissed me on the forehead, smiling a vague ghostly smile and placing one finger on her lips. I closed my eyes helplessly and plunged back into the mists of sleep. I woke up to see a ladder of bright dust motes reaching in from the balcony at the other end of the room. Concha was no longer by my side, but soon after that, the door slowly opened and Concha tiptoed in. I pretended to be asleep. She came closer, not making a sound; she looked at me, sighed, and placed in a vase the bunch of fresh roses she had brought me. She went over to the balcony and adjusted the curtains to keep out the light. Then she left as silently as she had come. I called out to her, laughing.

'Concha! Concha!'

She turned round.

'So you were awake, were you?'

'I was dreaming of you.'

'Well, here I am.'

'And how are you?'

'I'm fully recovered.'

'Love is the best doctor.'

'But we'd better not overdo the medicine.'

We lay in each other's arms, laughing happily, our mouths pressed together, our heads resting on the same pillow. Concha had the delicate, sickly pallor of a mater dolorosa, and she was so beautiful, so thin and wan, that my eyes, lips and hands found pleasure in the very things that saddened me. I confess I do not remember ever having loved her as madly as I did that night.

I had not taken a servant with me, and so Concha, imitating one of those princesses in picaresque stories, placed a page at my service, to do me greater honour, she said, laughing. He was a young boy whom Concha had taken in. I can see him now, peering round the door and removing his cap, asking in respectful, humble tones:

'May I?'

'Come in.'

He entered with his head bowed and a little white cloth cap clutched in his two hands.

'My lady says to ask if you need anything.'

'Where is she?'

'In the garden.'

And he stood in the middle of the room, not daring to take a step. I think he was the eldest child of the people who tended Concha's land in Lantañón and one of her uncle's one hundred godchildren; her uncle, Juan Manuel Montenegro, was the generous, visionary gentleman who lived in the great house at Lantañón. It still makes me smile to think of it. Concha's favourite was neither blond nor melancholy like the pages who appear in ballads, but with his dark eyes and bright cheeks honeyed by the sun, he too could have won a princess's heart. I ordered him to open the balcony doors, and he obeyed at the double. The cool, scented breeze blew in from the garden, making the curtains flutter gaily. The page had left his cap on a chair and he came back to pick it up. I asked him:

'Do you work in the palace?'

'Yes, sir.'

'Have you been here long?'

'Nearly two years.'

'And what do you do?'

'Whatever I'm asked to.'

'Do you have no mother and father?'

'I have, sir.'

'And what do they do?'

'They don't do anything. They just dig the earth.'

He gave the stoical replies of the downtrodden. In his serge clothes, with his shy eyes, his visigothic speech, his shock of hair chopped into a straight fringe, his almost monkish tonsure, he looked like the son of a former bondsman.

'And was it your lady herself who told you to come?'

'Yes, sir. I was down in the courtyard teaching the new blackbirds a song – because the old ones already know it – when the mistress came down to the garden and told me to come.'

'Are you in charge of training the blackbirds here?'

'Yes, sir.'

'And now you are also my page.'

'Yes, sir.'

'Important posts!'

'Yes, sir.'

'And how old are you?'

'I think . . . I think . . .' The page thought hard and stared down at his cap, passing it slowly from one hand to the other. 'I think I must be about twelve, but I'm not sure.'

'Where were you before you came to the palace?'

'I served in the house of Don Juan Manuel.'

'And what did you do there?'

'I trained the ferret.'

'Yet another courtly post!'

'Yes, sir.'

'And how many blackbirds does your mistress have?'

The page boy pulled a scornful face.

'None!'

'Who do the birds belong to, then?'

'They're mine. When I've trained them up, I sell them.'

'And who do you sell them to?'

'To my mistress, of course. She buys every one of them. She only wants them so that she can set them free again. She wants them to fly around the garden singing, but they end up miles away. One Sunday, in the month of San Juan, I was walking with the mistress and we had just passed the Lantañón meadows, when we saw one of my blackbirds perched high up on the branch of a cherry tree, singing its song. I remember what my lady said then, she said: 'Just look what a long way that gentleman has come."

The ingenuous tale made me laugh out loud, and when he saw me laughing, the page boy laughed too. He may not have been blond or melancholy, but he was worthy of being the page of a princess and the chronicler of a whole reign. I asked him:

'Which is the more honourable occupation, training ferrets or blackbirds?'

After considering for a moment, he replied:

'It's all the same really.'

'And why did you leave the service of Don Juan Manuel?'

'Because he already had a lot of servants. Don Juan Manuel is a great man, you know. All the servants were afraid of him. Don Juan Manuel is my godfather and he was the one who brought me to the palace to serve my mistress.'

'And where did you get on best?'

The page boy fixed me with dark, childish eyes and said, very gravely, still holding his cap in his hands:

'If you know your place, you get on well anywhere.'

It was a reply worthy of Calderón. That page certainly had a way with aphorisms. There was no doubting what his destiny would be. He was born to live in a palace, to train blackbirds and ferrets, to be the servant to a prince and to shape the heart of a great king.

Concha was calling to me cheerfully from the garden. I went out onto the balcony, which was warm and golden in the morning sunlight. There was something about the countryside – the yoked oxen, the grape harvests, the ploughed fields – that seemed very Latin. Concha was standing underneath my balcony.

'Have you got Florisel there?'

'The pageboy?'

'Yes.'

'He was obviously christened by the fairies.'

'And I'm his fairy godmother. Will you send him down to me?'

'What do you want from him?'

'I want him to bring you these roses.'

And Concha held out her skirt which was full of gathered roses losing their petals, still covered in dew, in joyous plenitude, like the imaginary fruit of a love that flowers only in kisses.

'They're all for you. I'm stripping the whole garden.'

I had a vague memory of that ancient garden where, around an abandoned fountain, centuries-old myrtle bushes had been clipped into the shapes of the founder's four coats of arms. The garden and the palace belonged to a noble, melancholy age in which people had led pleasant lives filled with gallantry and romance. Laughter and madrigals had once blossomed beneath the canopy of leaves in the maze, on the terraces and in the salons, when the white hands which, in old portraits, merely clutch lace handkerchiefs, were busy plucking the petals from daisies that guard the innocent secrets of people's hearts. Such beautiful, far-off memories! I too evoked them one distant day, when the golden autumn morning enveloped the garden still damp and green from the constant rain of the previous night. Beneath the clear, azure sky the venerable cypress trees seemed lost in a dream of monastic life. The caressing light trembled on the flowers like a golden bird, and on the velvet lawn the breeze traced imaginary, fantastical footsteps as if invisible fairies were dancing there. Concha was standing at the foot of the steps, absorbed in making a huge bouquet of roses. Some had dropped their petals in her lap and she showed them to me, smiling.

'Look, isn't it a pity!' And she pressed their velvet coolness to her pale cheeks. 'They have such a wonderful perfume!'

I smiled and said.

'It's your own divine perfume!'

She looked up and took a deep, delicious breath, closing her eyes and smiling, her face covered in dew, like one more rose – a white rose. Against that backdrop of graceful green shade, swathed in light as if in a diaphanous gown of gold, she looked like a Madonna as imagined by some seraphic monk. I went down to join her. As I came down the steps, she showered me with the fallen rose petals gathered in her skirt. Together we walked about the garden. The paths were covered in dry, yellowish leaves that sighed as the wind swept them along before us. The snails, motionless as arthritic old men, were enjoying the sun on the stone benches. The flowers were beginning to fade in the Versaillesque baskets embroidered with myrtle, and they gave off an elusive aroma redolent of sad memories. In the depths of the maze murmured a fountain surrounded by cypress trees, and the murmur of the water seemed to plunge the whole garden into a peaceful vision of old age, seclusion and neglect. Concha said to me:

'Let's stop here.'

We sat down in the shade of the acacia trees, on a stone bench covered with leaves. Opposite us was the entrance to the mysterious, green maze. Above the keystone of the arch were two moss-covered chimera, and a single, shady path wove through the myrtles like the path of a solitary life, silent and unknown. In the distance, Florisel walked by amongst the trees, carrying his cage of blackbirds in his hand. Concha pointed him out to me:

'There he goes!'

'Who?'

'Florisel.'

'Why do you call him Florisel?'

With a happy laugh she said:

'Florisel is the name of the pageboy with whom a certain inconsolable princess falls in love; I read about them in a story.'

'Whose story?'

'Stories don't belong to anyone.'

Her moody, mysterious eyes stared off into the distance and her laughter sounded so strange to me that I felt cold, the cold that comes from understanding all perversities. It seemed to me that Concha too was shivering. We were, after all, at the start of autumn and the clouds were beginning to cover the sky. We returned to the palace.

Although it had been built in the eighteenth century, the Palacio de Brandeso was designed almost entirely in the plateresque style of the sixteenth. A palace *a la italiana* with balconies, fountains and gardens, commissioned by the Bishop of Corinth, Don Pedro de Bendaña, a Knight of St James, a Commander of the Cross, and Confessor to Queen María Amelia de Parma. I believe that Concha's grandfather and my grandfather, Marshal Bendaña, were involved in a legal dispute over who should inherit the palace. I am not sure, though, because my grandfather was always involved in law suits, even with the Royal House itself, which is why I inherited a whole fortune in dossiers and files. The history of the noble house of Bendaña is the history of the crown court of Valladolid.

Poor Concha adored memories, and she wanted us to walk around the palace recalling the old days when I used to visit with my mother and when she and her sisters were still pale little girls who would greet me with a kiss and take me by the hand so that we could play together, sometimes in the tower, sometimes on the terrace, at others on the balcony that looked out over the road and the garden. That morning, as we were climbing the crumbling steps, the doves flew up and alighted on the carved stone coat of arms. The windows were golden in the sun, old wallflowers bloomed amongst the cracks in the wall and a lizard strolled along the balustrade. Concha smiled languidly.

'Do you remember?'

And I could sense the whole past in her subtle smile, the way the precious perfume of faded flowers brings with it a happy confusion of memories. That was where a sad and pious lady used to tell us stories about the saints. Sitting with me in a window seat, she had often shown me the holy pictures in *The Christian Year*, open on her lap. I still remember her noble, mystical hands slowly turning the pages. The lady had a lovely old-fashioned name: she was called Águeda. She

35

was the mother of Fernanda, Isabel and Concha, the three pale
little girls with whom I used to play. After all those years, I saw
again the salons reserved for special occasions and those other
familiar rooms, cold, silent rooms with walnut floors, rooms
that smelled all year round of the sour, autumn apples left to
ripen on the window sills, the salons with their ancient damask curtains, tarnished mirrors and family portraits: ladies in
full skirts, prelates with learned smiles, pale abbesses, grim
captains. In those rooms our footsteps echoed as in deserted
churches, and each time we gingerly opened another door
decorated with florid ironwork, the dark, silent depths
exhaled the distant aroma of other lives. Only in one room,
the floor of which was laid with cork, did our footsteps
awaken no echo at all – like the silent footsteps of ghosts. In
the mirrors the salon disappeared into a dream-like distance as
if in an enchanted lake, and the people in the portraits, those
founding bishops, those sad damsels, those desiccated eldest
sons, seemed to live forgotten in an ancient peace. Concha
stopped at the point where the two corridors met and opened
out into a round anteroom where, day and night, an oil lamp
lit a dishevelled, livid Christ figure. Concha murmured:

'Do you remember this anteroom?'

'The round one?'

'Yes, it was where we used to play.'

An old woman was sitting in the window seat spinning.
Concha pointed to her.

'It's Micaela, my mother's maidservant. The poor thing is
blind. Don't say anything to her.'

We continued on. Sometimes Concha would stop at an
open door and point silently in at the room, saying to me with
that vague smile of hers that also seemed to be dissolving into
the past:

'Do you remember?'

She remembered things that had happened years ago. She
remembered when we were children and used to jump up
and down in front of the console tables to make the
ornaments on them tremble: vases laden with roses, bell jars
placed over ancient arrangements of gilded branches, the

silver candelabra and the daguerreotypes full of starry wonder – the days when our mad, happy laughter had disturbed the stately silence of the palace and now died away in the large, bright anterooms, along dark corridors flanked by narrow mullioned windows in which doves were cooing.

When it grew dark, Concha felt terribly cold and had to lie down. I was so alarmed by her shivering, by her deathly pallor, that I wanted to send for the doctor in Viana del Prior, but she wouldn't let me, and after an hour, she was smiling up at me again, loving and languid. Lying motionless on the white pillows, she murmured:

'Can you believe that being ill seems a blessing to me now.'

'Why?'

'Because you're here taking care of me.'

I smiled but said nothing and she, with great sweetness, insisted:

'You have no idea how much I love you, do you?'

In the half-light of the bedroom, Concha's soft voice had a deep, sentimental charm that infected my very soul.

'Ah, but I love you more, princess.'

'No, before, you really did love me. However innocent a woman might be, that's something she always knows, and you know how innocent I was.'

I bent over to kiss her eyes, which were veiled with tears, and said, to console her:

'You don't honestly think I could have forgotten, do you, Concha?'

She exclaimed, laughing:

'You are an old cynic!'

'I'm just rather forgetful. It all happened a very long time ago you know.'

'How long? Tell me.'

'Don't make me sad remembering all the years that have passed.'

'But I *was* very innocent, wasn't I?'

'As innocent as any married woman can be.'

'I was much more innocent. You taught me everything.'

She almost sighed the last words and placed one hand over her eyes. I looked at her, feeling the voluptuous memory of the senses stir into life. Concha still retained for me all her former charms, only purified by the divine paleness of her illness. I had indeed taught her everything. As a child, married off to an old man, she had all the innocent awkwardness of a virgin. Some marriage beds are as cold as tombs, and some husbands sleep in them like recumbent granite statues. Poor Concha! On her lips perfumed by prayers, my lips were the first to sing the triumph of love and its glorious exaltation. I had to teach her the whole cycle, line by line, of Pietro Aretino's thirty-two sonnets. That lovely, white, unopened flower of a child bride could only mumble the very first. There are husbands and lovers who are not even useful as precursors and, God knows, the bloody rose of perversity, has never bloomed in my love affairs. I have always preferred to be the Marquis of Bradomín rather than the divine Marquis de Sade. Perhaps that is the reason why some women considered me proud, though Concha was never one of them. We had fallen silent and she said:

'What are you thinking about?'

'About the past, Concha.'

'I'm jealous of your past.'

'Don't be such a child. I was thinking about our past love.'

She smiled and closed her eyes as if she too were calling up some memory. Then she murmured in a tone of gentle resignation, sweet with love and melancholy:

'I have only ever asked Our Lady for one thing and I believe she is going to grant it to me – to have you by my side at the hour of my death.'

We again fell into a sad silence. After a while, Concha sat up amongst her pillows. Her eyes were full of tears. In a very low voice she said:

'Xavier, hand me the jewellery box that's on my dressing table. Open it. That's where I keep your letters too. Let's burn them together. I don't want them to survive me.'

It was a silver box, made with all the decadent lavishness of the eighteenth century. It gave off a sweet smell of violets, which I breathed in, closing my eyes.

'Haven't you got anyone else's letters in here?'

'No.'

'Ah, so your new lover doesn't know how to write.'

'My new lover? What new lover? I suppose you've dreamed up some dreadful atrocity?'

'I believe I have.'

'What?'

'I'm not telling you.'

'And what if I were to guess?'

'You can't.'

'What enormity have you invented?'

Laughing, I exclaimed:

'Florisel.'

A shadow of anger passed over Concha's eyes.

'How could you even think that?'

She plunged her fingers into my hair, ruffling it.

'What am I going to do with you? Shall I kill you?'

She laughed to see me laughing, and on her pale lips her laughter was fresh, sensual, joyous.

'You can't possibly have thought that.'

'Tell me it's impossible.'

'Did you really think that?'

'Yes.'

'I don't believe you. How could you even imagine such a thing?'

'I remembered my first conquest. I was eleven when a lady fell in love with me. She was very beautiful too.'

'My Aunt Augusta.'

'Yes.'

'You told me about that once. But weren't you handsomer than Florisel?'

I hesitated for a moment and almost besmirched my lips with a lie. In the end, though, I had the courage to confess the truth.

'No, Concha, I was much less handsome.'

She gave me a mocking look and closed the jewellery box.

'I'll burn your letters another day, not today. Your jealousy has put me in a good mood.'

And leaning back on her pillows, she burst out again in

peals of fresh, rapturous laughter. We never did burn those letters. I have always resisted burning love letters. I have loved them as a poet loves his poetry. When Concha died, her daughters inherited them along with the family jewels in the silver box.

Ailing, enamoured souls are perhaps those who weave the loveliest, most hope-filled dreams. I had never seen Concha happier, more joyful. That rebirth of our love was like a pleasant, melancholy autumn afternoon of golden skies – afternoons and skies that I could contemplate from the palace balconies, when Concha, feigning a romantic weariness, would lean upon my shoulder. The road wound away through the damp, green countryside beneath the dying sun. It was a bright, deserted road. Gazing into the distance, Concha sighed.

'That is the road we must both one day take.'

And she raised one pale hand to indicate the distant cypress trees in the cemetery. Poor Concha spoke of dying, though without really believing in it. I said jokingly:

'Now don't make me sad, Concha. You know perfectly well that I am an enchanted prince held captive in your palace by a spell. In order for the spell to remain unbroken, you have to make my life into a happy tale.'

Forgetting her twilight sadness, Concha was smiling again.

'It's also the road that brought you here.'

Poor Concha tried to look happy. She knew that all tears are bitter tears and that a sigh, even the gentlest and sweetest of sighs, should last only as long as a gust of wind. Poor Concha! She was as pale and white as those Madonna lilies which, as they fade, fill chapels with their delicate perfume. She again lifted her hand, diaphanous as the hand of a fairy.

'Can you see a rider over there in the distance?'

'I can't see anything.'

'He's just passing Fontela.'

'Yes, now I see him.'

'It's my uncle, Don Juan Manuel.'

'The magnificent lord of Lantañón manor!'

Concha pulled a sad face.

'Poor thing. I'm sure he's coming to see you.'

Don Juan Manuel had stopped in the middle of the road and was standing up in his stirrups and doffing his wide-brimmed hat to greet us. Then, in a powerful voice that received a distant echo, he cried:

'Niece! Tell them to open the garden gate!'

Concha raised her arms to indicate that she would, then, turning to me, she said, laughing:

'Tell him they're on their way.'

Cupping my mouth with my hands, I roared:

'They're coming!'

But Don Juan Manuel pretended not to hear me. The privilege of making oneself heard at that distance was his alone. Concha put her hands over her ears.

'Shh, he'll never admit that he can hear you.'

I continued roaring:

'They're coming! They're coming!'

In vain. Don Juan Manuel leaned forward to pat his horse's neck. He had resolved not to hear me. Then he stood up in his stirrups again.

'Niece! Niece!'

Concha leaned on the window, laughing like a happy child.

'Isn't he magnificent!'

And the old man kept shouting from the road:

'Niece! Niece!'

He really was magnificent. He obviously judged that the gate was not being opened to him with sufficient speed, for he dug his spurs into his horse and galloped off. From afar, he turned and shouted:

'Can't stop, I'm off to Viana del Prior. There's a scrivener there who needs to be taught a lesson.'

Florisel, who had run down to open the gate, stopped to watch this elegant departure. Then he came back up the worn steps, overgrown with ivy. As he passed us, he said in solemn, learned tones, without looking up:

'He's a great man, Don Juan Manuel, a very great man indeed.'

I think he meant it as a criticism of us, because we were laughing at the old man. I called out to him:

'Hey, Florisel!'

Trembling, he stopped.

'Yes, sir.'

'Do you really think Don Juan Manuel is such a great man?'

'Present company excepted, sir.'

And his childish eyes, fixed on Concha, begged forgiveness. Concha made an indulgent, queenly gesture, only to spoil it all by laughing like a mad thing. Florisel moved off in silence. We kissed each other joyfully and, as we kissed, we heard the distant singing of the blackbirds, led by Florisel on his bamboo flute.

It was a moonlit night and, in the depths of the maze, the fountain was singing like a hidden bird. We were sitting in silence, holding hands. In the middle of that meditative quiet, we heard the sound of slow, weary footsteps coming down the corridor. Candelaria came in carrying a lamp and Concha cried out as if she had been woken from a dream.

'Take that light away!'

'Do you mean you want to be in the dark? You shouldn't sit in the moonlight, you know, it's bad for you.'

Concha asked, smiling:

'And why is that, Candelaria?'

The old woman lowered her voice:

'You know perfectly well why, señorita . . . because of witches.'

Candelaria took the lamp away again, crossing herself repeatedly, while we went back to listening to the song of the fountain which was telling the moon of its imprisonment in the maze. A cuckoo clock, which had belonged to the founder of the house, struck seven. Concha murmured:

'It gets dark so early now! It's only seven o'clock.'

'Winter's on its way.'

'When do you have to leave?'

'Me? When you allow me to.'

Concha sighed.

'When I allow you to indeed. If I had my way, you would never leave.'

And she silently squeezed my hand. From our place on the balcony we could see the garden lit by the moon, the faded cypresses crowned with stars against the blue night sky, and a black fountain with silver water. Concha said:

'I received a letter yesterday. I must show it to you.'

'A letter? From whom?'

'From our cousin Isabel. She's coming here and she's bringing the girls with her.'

'Isabel Bendaña?'

'Yes.'

'Has Isabel got daughters then?'

Concha said shyly:

'No, they're mine.'

I felt an April breeze blow over the garden of my memories. Once, those two girls, Concha's daughters, had been very fond of me and I of them. I looked up at their mother. I had never before seen such a sad smile on Concha's lips.

'What's wrong? Are you all right?'

'It's nothing.'

'Do they live with their father?'

'No, they're being educated at the Convento de la Enseñanza.'

'They must be nearly grown up.'

'They're certainly very tall.'

'They used to be very pretty. I don't know what they'll be like now.'

'Like their mother.'

'No, they could never be like their mother.'

Concha smiled that same sad smile and sat looking thoughtfully down at her hands.

'I have to ask you a favour.'

'What?'

'If Isabel comes with my daughters, we have to put on a little act. I'll tell them that you're in Lantañón hunting with my uncle. You will just happen to come over one afternoon and, either because there's a storm or because we're afraid of intruders, you can stay on at the palace, as our knight.'

'And how long must I be exiled in Lantañón?'

Concha exclaimed quickly:

'No time at all. Only on the actual afternoon they arrive. You're not offended, are you?'

'No, my love.'

'I'm so glad. I've been worrying about it since yesterday, not daring to tell you.'

'Do you think we'll deceive Isabel?'

'I'm not doing it for Isabel's benefit, but for my two little girls, who are almost young women now.'

'And what about Don Juan Manuel?'

'I'll talk to him. He has no scruples about such things. He's another descendant of the Borgias. He's your uncle too, isn't he?'

'I don't know. Perhaps I'm related to him through you.'

She replied, laughing:

'I don't think so. I have an idea that your mother used to call him cousin.'

'Oh, my mother knows the story behind the whole family tree. Now, we'll have to consult Florisel.'

'He will be our king-of-arms.'

A smile trembled on the pale rose of her mouth. Then she grew pensive and sat looking out at the garden, her hands folded in her lap. In their bamboo cage hanging by the balcony door, Florisel's blackbirds were whistling an old song. In the silence of the night, that bright, country melody evoked memories of happy Celtic dances danced in the shade of ancient oak trees. Concha began to sing too. Her voice was soft as a caress. She got up and wandered about the balcony. Then, standing at the far end, all white in the moonlight, she began to dance one of those jolly pastoral dances, only to stop, breathing hard:

'Ooph, I get so tired. You see, I've learned the song as well!'

I laughed and said:

'So you're one of Florisel's pupils too?'

'I am.'

I went over to help her. She put her hands on my shoulders and, resting her cheek on my chest, she looked up at me with beautiful, fevered eyes. I kissed her and she bit my lips with her pale lips.

Poor Concha! Though drawn and pale, she had the noble stamina for pleasure of a goddess. That night the flame of passion wrapped its golden tongue about us for a long time, first dying down, then blazing up again. I fell asleep in Concha's arms, listening to the singing of the birds in the garden. When I woke, she was sitting up against the pillows, with such a look of pain and suffering on her face, that I went cold. Poor Concha! When she saw me open my eyes, she smiled though. Stroking her hands, I asked:

'What's wrong?'

'I don't know. I feel really ill.'

'What's wrong?'

'I don't know, it would be so shameful if I were to be found dead here!'

When I heard her say that, I felt an immediate desire to keep her by my side.

'You're shivering, poor love!'

I held her in my arms. She half-closed her eyes. They closed like that when she wanted me to kiss them. She was trembling so much that I tried to warm her whole body with my lips, and my mouth moved conscientiously along her arms to her shoulders and placed a necklace of roses about her neck. Then I looked up at her. She folded her pale hands and looked at them sadly – poor delicate, bloodless, almost fragile hands. I said to her:

'You have the hands of a mater dolorosa.'

She smiled.

'I have the hands of a dead woman.'

'As far as I'm concerned, the paler you are the more beautiful.'

Joy flashed in her eyes.

'Yes, you're still very drawn to me; I still move you.'

She put one arm about my neck and with her other hand lifted her breasts – snow roses consumed by fever. I held her close and, even in the midst of desire, I was gripped by the terror of being there at her death. When I heard her sigh, I thought she was dying. I kissed her, trembling, as if I were about to suck the life from her. With a sad voluptuousness, such as I had never known before, my soul grew drunk on that perfume, the perfume of a dying flower from which my devoted, impious fingers tore the petals. Her eyes opened and looked lovingly up into mine, but there was still great suffering in them. The following day Concha was too ill to leave her bed.

The afternoon was slipping away amidst a shower of rain. I had taken refuge in the library and was reading *A Florilegium for Our Lady*, a book of sermons by the Bishop of Corinth, Don Pedro de Bendaña, the founder of the palace. Sometimes I amused myself listening to the roar of the wind in the garden and the whisper of dry leaves tumbling along the avenues of ancient myrtle bushes. The bare branches of the trees scraped against the panes of the leaded windows. A monastic peace reigned in the library, as in some canonical, learned dream. In the air could be felt the breath of old folios bound in parchment, the books on the humanities and on theology that the Bishop had studied. Suddenly, I heard a loud voice calling from outside in the corridor.

'Marquis! Marquis!'

I placed the book face down on the table, to keep my place, and stood up. Just at that moment, the door opened and Don Juan Manuel appeared on the threshold, shaking the wet from his cape.

'Terrible afternoon, nephew!'

'Terrible, uncle!'

And thus our kinship was sealed.

'What are you doing shut up in here reading? You'll ruin your eyesight.'

He went over to the fire and held out his hands to the flames.

'It's snowing out there now!'

Then he turned his back to the fire and, standing before me, exclaimed in his affected, lordly voice:

'Nephew, you have inherited your grandfather's mania. He used to spend all day reading too. That's why he went mad. And what great fat tome is that?'

With his sunken, greenish eyes he gave the book a look of utter scorn. He left the fireside and took a few steps about the library, making his spurs ring. Then he stopped.

'Marquis, has the palace's supply of Christ's blood entirely run dry?'

Realising what he meant, I got to my feet. Don Juan Manuel stretched out an arm, holding me back with a sovereign gesture.

'Don't move. I imagine there must be a servant somewhere in the palace.'

And from the far end of the library he started bawling:

'Arnelas! Brión! Anyone! Come at once!'

He was just beginning to grow impatient when Florisel appeared at the door.

'Do you need anything, sir?'

And he went and kissed Don Juan Manuel's hand, and Don Juan Manuel, in turn, stroked Florisel's head.

'Bring me up some of that red wine from Fontela.'

And he began pacing up and down the library again. From time to time he stopped to hold out his hands to the fire; he had the pale, gaunt, aristocratic hands of an ascetic king. Despite the years, which had left his hair completely white, he was still as erect and arrogant as he had been in his prime when he served in the royal guard. He had retired many years before to his manor house in Lantañón, leading the typical life of the eldest son of any rural, land-owning family: haggling at fairs, gambling in towns and, at every fiesta, sitting at the priests' table. Since Concha had been living at the Palacio de Brandeso, he had been a frequent visitor there too. He would tether his horse at the garden gate and stride up to the house, shouting. He would call for wine and drink himself to sleep in his armchair. When he woke, regardless of whether it was day or night, he would call for his horse and ride back home, nodding in the saddle. Don Juan Manuel had a great liking for the red wine of Fontela, kept in a huge cask that dated back to the days of the French. Growing impatient because they were taking their time in bringing it up from the cellar, he stood in the middle of the library and bawled:

'Where's that wine? Or are they still picking the grapes?'

Trembling, Florisel appeared with a jug, which he placed

on the table. Don Juan Manuel removed his coat and sat down in an armchair.

'I can promise you, Marquis, this Fontela wine is the best wine in the region. Do you know the wine from Condado? Well, this is better. And if they were more careful in their choice of grapes, it would be the best in the world.'

He was saying all this while pouring out some wine into a cut-glass goblet with a handle, and the cross of Calatrava engraved in the bottom. It was one of those heavy, antique glasses that remind one of convent refectories. Don Juan Manuel drank the wine down in one long, slow draught, then refilled his glass.

'If my niece drank a few more glasses of this, she wouldn't be in the state she's in now.'

Just then, a smiling Concha appeared at the door of the library, dragging behind her the train of her monastic dressing gown.

'Don Juan Manuel wants you to go back with him, did he tell you? Tomorrow is the big fiesta there: San Rosendo de Lantañón. My uncle says you will receive a royal welcome.'

Don Juan Manuel nodded magnanimously.

'As you know, for three centuries it has been the privilege of the Marquises of Bradomín to be received thus in the parishes of San Rosendo de Lantañón, Santa Baya de Cristamilde and San Miguel de Deiro. If I'm not mistaken, the three curacies are in the gift of your family. Or am I wrong, nephew?'

'No, you're quite right, uncle.'

Concha interrupted, laughing.

'There's no point asking him. Sad to say, the latest Marquis of Bradomín doesn't know a thing about such matters.'

Don Juan Manual shook his head gravely.

'Surely he knows that – at least he should.'

Concha dropped down into the armchair that I had been sitting in shortly before and, with a learned air, opened the book I had been reading.

'I don't think he even knows the origin of the house of Bradomín.'

Don Juan Manuel turned to me and said in a gracious, conciliatory tone:

'Take no notice. Your cousin is just trying to provoke you.'

Concha insisted:

'He doesn't even know the coat of arms of the noble house of Montenegro.'

Don Juan Manuel knit his brows.

'Even little children know that.'

Concha murmured, with a smile of sweet, delicate irony:

'After all, it is the most illustrious of Spanish lineages.'

'Spanish and German, niece. The Montenegros of Galicia descend from a German empress. It is the only Spanish coat of arms to have metal on metal: golden spurs on a field of silver. The Bradomín line is equally ancient. But of all the titles in your family: the Marquisate of Bradomín, the Marquisate of San Miguel, the Earldom of Barbanzón and the Lordship of Padín, the last is the oldest and most distinguished. That goes back to Roland, one of the twelve peers. As you know, Roland did not die in Roncesvalles, as the history books say.'

I knew nothing about this, but Concha nodded. She was doubtless aware of that family secret. After downing another glass of wine, Don Juan Manuel went on:

'I know about these things because I too am descended from Roland. Roland managed to escape and he boarded a ship that took him as far as the Isle of Sálvora, where he was shipwrecked, lured onto the beach by a siren. That siren bore him a son, who, being Roland's son, was called Padín, which means paladin. And that is why, in the church of Lantañón, a siren is shown embracing and supporting your coat of arms.'

He got to his feet and, going over to the window, looked out to see if the weather was improving. The sun could only be glimpsed through dense clouds. For a while, Don Juan Manuel remained gazing up at the sky. Then he turned back to us:

'I'm just going up to inspect my mills over there, then I'll come back to get you. Since you're so keen on reading, when we get to my house, I'll give you an old book to read, one with nice, large, clear print, in which all these stories are recounted in full.'

Don Juan Manuel drained his glass and left the library, his spurs jingling. When the sound of his footsteps had disappeared down the long corridor, Concha, leaning heavily on the arms of her chair, got up and came over to me. She was white as a ghost.

In the depths of the maze, the fountain was singing like a hidden bird, and the setting sun was gilding the windows of the balcony where we were waiting. It was warm and fragrant there. Graceful arches, filled by stained-glass windows, flanked the balcony doors with the consummate artifice of the gallant century that created the pavanne and the gavotte. In each arch, the stained-glass windows formed a triptych and through them one could see the garden in the middle of a thunder storm, in the middle of a snow storm and beneath a shower of rain. That evening, the autumn sun was piercing the central window like the weary lance of a hero of old.

Standing motionless in the doorway, Concha was watching the road and sighing. Doves fluttered about her. Poor Concha was annoyed with me because I had laughed at her story of a heavenly apparition that had come to her while she was asleep in my arms. It was a dream such as saints have in those stories told to me when I was a child by the sad, pious lady who then lived in the palace. I vaguely remember that dream. Concha was lost in the maze, sitting at the foot of the fountain and crying inconsolably. At that moment, an archangel appeared. He was carrying neither sword nor buckler. He was as pale and melancholy as a lily. Concha realised that this adolescent had not come in order to do battle with Satan. She smiled at him through her tears and the archangel spread his wings of light above her and guided her out of the maze. The maze was the sin in which Concha was lost, and the waters of the fountain were the tears that she would have to cry in Purgatory. Despite our love, Concha would not be damned. After guiding her past the still, green myrtles at the archway on which the two chimera stood face to face, the archangel flapped his wings in order to fly away. Concha knelt down and asked him if she should enter a convent; the archangel gave no answer. Wringing her hands, Concha asked if she should tear the petals from the flower of her love and cast them to the winds;

the archangel gave no answer. Dragging herself across the flagstones, she asked him if she was going to die; the archangel gave no answer, but Concha felt two tears fall on her hands. The tears rolled between her fingers like two diamonds. Then Concha understood the mystery of that dream. When she told me the story, she sighed, poor thing, and said to me:

'It's a warning from Heaven, Xavier.'

'Dreams are never anything more than dreams, Concha.'

'I'm going to die. Don't you believe in apparitions?'

I smiled because at the time I did not, and Concha walked slowly over to the balcony door. The doves fluttered above her like a happy omen. The lush, green countryside smiled in the peace of the afternoon, with the scattered houses of the villages and the distant windmills half-hidden behind the vine trellises at their doors, and with the blue mountains topped by the first snows. Beneath the pleasant sun that shone between the showers, the village people were out walking along the roads. A shepherdess wearing a red shawl was leading her sheep towards the church of San Gundián, women were returning from the fountain singing, a weary old man was goading on his yoke of cattle which had stopped by the fence to graze, and white smoke seemed to curl up from amongst the fig trees. The glorious, magnificent figure of Don Juan Manuel appeared at the top of the hill, his cape fluttering behind him. At the foot of the stairs, Brión, the steward, was holding by the reins an old horse which was as prudent, thoughtful and grave as a pontiff. The horse was white with a long, venerable mane, and had been in the palace since time immemorial. It neighed proudly and, when she heard it, Concha wiped away a tear that made her mortal eyes seem even more beautiful.

'Will you come back tomorrow, Xavier?'

'I will.'

'Do you swear?'

'I do.'

'You're not angry with me?'

Smiling slightly mockingly, I said:

'No, I'm not angry with you, Concha.'

And we kissed each other in the romantic way of other times. I was the crusader leaving for Jerusalem and Concha was the lady left weeping in her castle in the moonlight. I must confess that as long as I wore my hair long like Espronceda and Zorrilla, in the style of the Merovingian kings, I could never bring myself to say goodbye in any other way. Now that the years have left me with a tonsure more befitting a deacon, I can only allow myself to murmur a melancholy farewell. A happy time, the time of youth. If only we could be like that fountain which, in the depths of the maze, still laughs its crystalline laugh, soulless and ageless.

From behind the glass panes of the balcony door, Concha was saying goodbye to us, waving one white hand. The sun had still not set and the graceful crescent of the moon was already beginning to shine in the sad, autumnal sky. It was two leagues to the house at Lantañón, and the bridleway was stony and full of large pools, before which our horses would pause, twitching their ears, whilst, on the other side, some village lad would stand watching us in silence, placidly letting his weary oxen drink. The shepherds returning from the hills, driving their flocks before them, waited at the passing places and kept their sheep to one side in order to let us through. Don Juan Manuel went first. He kept lurching about on his horse which seemed restless and unaccustomed to the saddle. It was a wild dapple grey, not many hands high, with fierce eyes and a hard mouth; its master seemed to have punished it by cropping its tail and mane. Don Juan Manuel rode it mercilessly. He dug his spurs in, at the same time pulling on the reins, causing the horse to rear up, though it never managed to unseat its master, because the old nobleman showed remarkable horsemanship.

We were still only halfway there when night fell. Don Juan Manuel continued lurching this way and that in the saddle, but that did not stop him booming out orders to me whenever we came to a rough patch in the road, telling me to rein in my nag. We reached a junction where three roads met and where a small altar had been built. A small group of women were kneeling there in prayer and they suddenly stood up, startling Don Juan Manuel's horse, which wheeled about and threw off its rider. The women cried out and the horse, rushing past them, broke into a gallop, dragging Don Juan Manuel with it, his foot trapped in the stirrup. I raced after him. There was a dull thwack as the brambles on either side of the road beat against Don Juan Manuel's body. The stony slope led down to the river and in the darkness I could see the sparks thrown up by the horse's shoes. At last, by actually riding over

Don Juan Manuel, I managed to get in front and position my horse across the road. His horse stopped short, covered in sweat and neighing, its sides heaving. I jumped down. Don Juan Manuel was smeared with blood and mud. When I bent over him, he slowly opened sad, glazed eyes. Without a word of complaint, he closed them again and I realised that he had fainted. I lifted him up, placed him across my horse and we set off back down the road. Near the palace I had to stop because Don Juan Manuel's body kept sliding off and I had to position him better on the saddle. The coldness of his hands hanging inertly down frightened me. I again took up the reins of my horse and we continued on to the palace. Despite the darkness, I could see three young men on mules riding out on to the road through the garden gate. From some way away, I shouted:

'Have you just delivered some guests to the palace?''

The three chorused:

'Yes, sir.'

'Who?'

'A youngish lady and two little girls. They arrived in Viana this very afternoon on the boat from Flavia-Longa.'

The three men held their mules in check by the side of the road, to let me pass. When they saw Don Juan Manuel's body slung over my horse, they muttered to each other. They did not, however, dare to question me. They must have presumed that it was someone I had killed, for I would swear that all three were shaking in their saddles. I stopped halfway along and ordered one of them to jump down and hold my horse, while I went up and warned the palace. He did so in silence. When I handed him the reins, he recognised Don Juan Manuel.

'Holy Mother of God, it's the lord of Lantañón.'

With trembling hand he took the reins and said in a low voice, full of awed respect:

'Has some misfortune happened, Marquis?'

'He fell off his horse.'

'It looks as if he's dead.'

'It does indeed.'

At that moment, Don Juan Manuel raised himself wearily up.

'Only half-dead, nephew.'

He sighed with all the fortitude of a man suppressing a groan, gave the men an inquisitorial look and then, turning to me, said:

'Who are these people?'

'The muleteers who brought Isabel and the girls.'

'Where are we then?'

'Near the palace.'

As we talked, I took up the horse's reins again and we walked down the ancient avenue. The muleteers said goodbye:

'A very good night to you!'

'Have a safe journey!'

'May the Lord be with you!'

They moved off at a stately pace on their mules. Don Juan Manuel gave a sigh and turned round; then, resting both hands on the pommel of the saddle, and even though the men were already some way off, he shouted to them in his usual commanding tones:

'If you find my horse, take him to Viana del Prior.'

A voice lost in the silence of the night, fragmented by the buffeting wind, replied:

'Don't worry, sir, don't worry!'

Beneath the familiar shade of the chestnut trees, my horse, scenting the stable, neighed again. In the distance, keeping close to the walls of the palace, two servants were talking in dialect. The one in front was carrying a lantern that swayed, slow and rhythmic. Behind the dew-misted glass of the lantern, the smoky flame from the oil lit up the wet earth and the villagers' clogs with tremulous clarity. Speaking in low voices, they stopped for a moment at the steps and, when they recognised us, came forward with the lantern raised high to light our way from afar. They were the two shepherds in charge of filling the mangers with the night's ration of damp, fragrant grass. They approached – clumsily, tentatively respectful – and lifted Don Juan Manuel down from my horse. They had placed the lantern on the balustrade of the steps, and from there it illumined the scene. Don Juan Manuel climbed up the steps, leaning heavily on the shoulders of the two servants, and I went ahead to warn Concha. She was such a good soul that she seemed always almost to be expecting some disaster.

I found Concha at her dressing table with her two daughters, engaged in combing the long hair of the youngest of them; the other was sitting on the Louis XV sofa beside her mother. The two girls were very similar; indeed, with their blonde hair and golden eyes, they looked like two young princesses painted by Titian in his old age. The elder of the two was called María Fernanda and the younger María Isabel. They were both talking at once about the events of the journey, and their mother smiled as she listened to them, delighted and happy, her pale fingers lost amongst the gold of their childish hair. When I went in, she started slightly, but soon controlled herself. The two young girls were looking at me, blushing bright red. The mother exclaimed in a somewhat shaken voice:

'How lovely to see you. Have you come from Lantañón? You probably heard that my daughters had arrived.'

'I heard about it when I got here. I owe the honour of seeing you to Don Juan Manuel, who fell off his horse going down the hill from Brandeso.'

The two girls asked their mother:

'Is that our uncle in Lantañón?'

'Yes, children.'

Concha left the ivory comb in her daughter's hair and, removing her pale hand from amongst the golden threads, silently held it out to me. The children's innocent eyes never left us for a moment. Their mother murmured:

'Good heavens, a fall at his age. And where were you coming from?'

'From Viana del Prior.'

'How is it that you didn't meet Isabel and my daughters on the way?'

'We came across country.'

Concha looked away so as not to laugh and continued combing her daughter's unplaited hair, the hair of a Venetian

62

matron falling over the shoulders of a child. Shortly afterwards, Isabel came in:

'Cousin, I knew you were here!'

'How did you know?'

'Because I saw Uncle Juan Manuel. It really is a miracle he wasn't killed.'

Concha got up, leaning on her daughters, who staggered a little under her weight and smiled as if it were a game.

'The poor man! Let's go and see him, my dears.'

I said to her:

'Leave it until tomorrow, Concha.'

Isabel went over to her and made her sit down.

'The best thing for you is to rest. We've applied vinegar poultices to his bruises, and Candelaria and Florisel have put him to bed.'

We all sat down. Concha told the eldest of her daughters to call Candelaria. The little girl jumped to her feet and ran to the door. When she got there, her mother said:

'Where are you going, María Fernanda?'

'Didn't you tell me to . . .'

'Yes, my dear, but you just have to bang the gong next to the dressing table.'

Slightly embarrassed, María Fernanda obeyed swiftly. Her mother kissed her tenderly and then, smiling, kissed the youngest, who was looking up at her with great topaz-coloured eyes. Candelaria came in unravelling a piece of white cloth, the threads of which would be made into balls for cleaning wounds.

'Did you call?'

María Fernanda stepped forward.

'I did, Candela. Mama told me to.'

And the girl ran to meet the old maidservant, taking the cloth from her hand so that she could continue unravelling it. María Isabel, who was sitting on the carpet with her head resting on her mother's knees, looked soulfully up:

'Candela, give it to me so that I can do it.'

'First come first served, my dear.'

And Candelaria, with the kindly smile of an old family

servant, held out her empty, wrinkled hands. María Fernanda went back to sit on the sofa. Then my cousin Isabel, who favoured the youngest, took the piece of linen, which still smelled of the countryside, and tore it in two.

'Here you are, my dear.'

Shortly afterwards, María Fernanda, placing thread upon thread on her lap, murmured, as grave as a grandmother:

'Spoiled little madam.'

Candelaria was still standing in the middle of the room awaiting orders, her hands folded over her crisp white apron. Concha asked after Don Juan Manuel.

'Have you left him alone now?'

'Yes, my lady. He's dozed off.'

'And where have you put him?'

'In the garden room.'

'We must prepare some rooms for the Marquis too. We can't have him going back alone to Lantañón.'

And poor Concha smiled at me with that ideal smile, the smile of the invalid. Her former nursemaid blushed scarlet to the roots of her hair. Then she looked tenderly at the children and murmured with all the old-fashioned severity of a devout, scrupulous duenna:

'The Bishop's rooms have already been prepared for the Marquis.'

She withdrew in silence. The two little girls continued to unravel the piece of cloth, casting furtive glances at each other to see who was doing most. Concha and Isabel were talking in whispers. The clock struck ten, and in the children's laps, in the luminous circle cast by the lamp, the threads were slowly forming a small white clump.

I sat down near the fire and passed the time stirring the logs with a pair of old, intricately carved, bronze tongs. The two girls had fallen asleep, the eldest with her head resting on her mother's shoulder, the youngest in my cousin Isabel's arms. Outside you could hear the rain beating against the windows and the wind gusting through the dark, mysterious garden. Ruby-red embers glowed in the fireplace, and, from time to time, a light, vivid flame licked about them.

So as not to wake the girls, Concha and Isabel continued talking in low voices. Not having seen one another for such a long time, both had their eyes turned to the past and were remembering far-off things. There was a long, whispered commentary about ancient, forgotten clan members. They spoke of the various aches and pains suffered by devout, ancient aunts, of pale cousins who had never married, of that poor Condesa de Cela who fell madly in love with a student, of Amelia Camarasa who died of consumption, of the Marquis of Tor who had fathered at least twenty-seven bastard children. They spoke of our noble and venerable uncle, the Bishop of Mondoñedo, that charitable saint who had taken into his palace the widow of a Carlist general, the King's aide-de-camp. However, I was barely listening to what Isabel and Concha were saying. From time to time, though, after ignoring me for long intervals, they would ask a question.

'Perhaps you'll know. How old is our uncle the bishop?'

'He must be about seventy.'

'That's what I said.'

'I'd have said he was older.'

And the warm, easy murmur of female conversation would start up again, until they asked me another question.

'Can you remember when my sisters took their vows?'

Concha and Isabel took me for the family chronicler. And so the evening passed. At about midnight, the conversation gradually died down, like the fire in the grate. After a long silence, Concha sat up with a weary sigh and tried to waken María Fernanda, who had gone to sleep on her shoulder.

'Come on, my love, I'm going to have to move you.'

María Fernanda opened her eyes, heavy with the innocent, adorable sleep of children. Her mother bent over to pick up the watch that she kept in her jewel box, along with her rings and the rosary.

'Gone midnight and the children are still up! Don't go back to sleep, my dear.'

And she tried to get María Fernanda to sit up, but the child was now resting her head on one arm of the sofa.

'We'll have you in bed in a minute.'

And with the smile fading on the withered rose of her mouth, Concha sat there looking at the youngest of her daughters sleeping in Isabel's arms, her long hair loose, like an angel buried in waves of gold.

'Poor little thing, it seems such a shame to wake her.'

And turning to me, she said:

'Would you mind calling Candelaria, Xavier?'

At the same time, Isabel tried to get up, still holding the child.

'I can't, she's too heavy.'

She smiled, admitting defeat, her eyes fixed on mine. I went over and carefully picked the little girl up without waking her. The wave of gold spilled over my shoulder. At that moment, we heard the slow steps of Candelaria coming down the corridor to carry the children off to bed.

When she saw me with María Isabel in my arms, she came over and said with a kind of familiar respect:

'I'll take her, Marquis. Don't you bother.'

And she smiled, with the kindly, placid smile one finds on the toothless mouths of old ladies. Silently, so as not to wake the little girl, I gestured to her to stop. My cousin Isabel got up and took María Fernanda by the hand; she was crying because her mother was putting her to bed. Her mother kissed her and said:

'You don't want to upset Isabel, do you?' And Concha looked at us hesitantly, wanting to please her daughter: 'Now do you?'

The little girl turned to Isabel with pleading, sleepy eyes.
'Are you upset?'
'I'm so upset that I certainly wouldn't stay here to sleep.'
With earnest curiosity, the little girl asked:
'Where would you go and sleep then?'
'Where else but in the priest's house!'

The little girl knew that the only possible place for a lady of the Bendaña family to stay was in the Palacio de Brandeso, and so, with sad eyes, she said goodnight to her mother. Concha remained alone at the dressing table. When we returned from the room where the children were sleeping, we found Concha crying. Isabel said to me in a low voice:

'She's more in love with you every day.'

Concha suspected that she was saying something else to me and she looked at us through her tears with jealous eyes. Isabel pretended not to notice. Smiling, she went in ahead of me and sat down on the sofa next to Concha.

'What's wrong, cousin?'

Concha did not reply, she merely dabbed at her eyes with her handkerchief and then tore at it with her teeth. I gave her a subtle, knowing smile and saw the roses bloom in her cheeks.

As I was closing the door of the room that served as my bedroom, I noticed a white shadow walking slowly along at the far end of the corridor, keeping close to the wall. It was Concha. She approached noiselessly.

'Are you alone, Xavier?'

'Alone with my thoughts, Concha.'

'That makes for bad company.'

'How did you guess? I was thinking of you.'

Concha paused at the door. Despite the look of fear in her eyes, she still managed a feeble smile. She glanced back along the dark corridor and trembled, terribly pale.

'I saw a black spider running across the floor. It was huge. It may still be caught up in my robe.'

She shook her long white train. Then we went into my room, silently closing the door. Concha stopped in the middle of the room and held out a letter that she drew from her bosom.

'It's from your mother.'

'For you or for me?'

'For me.'

She gave it to me, covering her eyes with one hand. I saw that she was biting her lips in order not to cry. Finally, she burst into sobs.

'Oh my God, oh my God.'

'What does she have to say?'

Concha pressed her hands to her forehead, which was almost obscured by a lock of black hair, tragic and austere, spreading like the dark smoke from a torch in the wind.

'Read it, read it! She says I'm the worst of women, that I live a scandalous life, that I'm damned, that I'm stealing her son from her . . .'

I calmly burned the letter in the flame of one of the candles. Concha groaned:

'I wanted you to read it.'

'No, my dear. She has such appalling handwriting.'

Seeing the letter reduced to ashes, poor Concha dried her tears.

'It's so awful that Aunt Soledad should write to me like that, when I love her and respect her so. That she should hate me, curse me, when all I want is to care for her and serve her as if I were her daughter. God, why am I so punished! Fancy saying that I bring you nothing but misfortune.'

I did not need to read my mother's letter, I could imagine it, I knew her style – desperate, furious clamourings, full of biblical references, like the curses uttered by a sibyl. I had received so many similar letters. The poor woman was a saint. The only reason she does not appear on any altars is because she was the first-born child and felt it her duty to perpetuate the family coat of arms, which was as illustrious as that of Don Juan Manuel. Had she had an elder brother to lay claim to the title, she would have entered a convent and become one of those peculiarly Spanish saints, an abbess and a visionary, a warrior and a fanatic.

For many years my mother – María Soledad Carlota Elena Agar y Bendaña – had led a devout, reclusive life in the Palacio de Bradomín. She was a very tall, grey-haired woman, charitable, credulous and despotic in the extreme. I used to visit her every autumn. She was full of aches and pains, but the sight of me, her eldest son, always seemed to revive her. She spent her days spinning for her servants, sitting in the window seat of a great balcony on a chair upholstered in crimson velvet with silver studs. In the afternoons, the sun would penetrate the depths of the room, tracing golden paths of light like the wake left behind by the holy visions she had experienced as a child. In the silence you could hear, day and night, the distant murmur of the river flowing into the millpond that served our mills. My mother spent hours and hours spinning on a distaff made of fine, perfumed lignum vitae. There was always the vague tremor of a prayer on her dry lips. She blamed Concha for all my troubles and held her in horror. She remembered as an eternal affront to her grey hairs the fact that our love affair had begun in the Palacio de Bradomín, during one summer

69

that Concha had spent there, keeping her company. My mother was her godmother and, at the time, loved her dearly. After that, she never saw her again. One day, when I was out hunting, Concha left the palace for ever. She left alone and weeping, with her head covered, like the heretics expelled from ancient Spanish cities by the Inquisition. My mother stood at the other end of the corridor, hurling curses at her, and beside my mother stood a pale maidservant, with downcast eyes – the betrayer of our love. Perhaps the same lips had told my mother now that I was at the Palacio de Brandeso. Concha kept saying over and over:

'Why am I so punished . . . why am I so punished!'

Round tears slid down her cheeks, bright and calm as the glass beads from a broken necklace or bracelet. Her voice faltered. My lips drank the tears from her eyes, her cheeks, from the corners of her mouth. Concha leaned her head on my shoulder, sighing; she was icy cold.

'She'll write to you as well. What will you do?'

I murmured in her ear:

'Whatever you want me to do.'

She fell silent and stood for a moment with her eyes closed. Then, opening them again, her eyes heavy now with a loving, resigned sadness, she sighed:

'If she does write to you, then do as your mother bids . . .'

She got up to leave. I stopped her.

'You're not saying what you really feel, Concha.'

'Yes I am. You see how I offend my husband every single day of my life. Well, I swear to you that, at the hour of my death, I would rather have your mother's forgiveness than his.'

'You will have everyone's forgiveness, Concha. And a papal blessing too.'

'If only God could hear you, but God can hear neither of us.'

'We'll get Don Juan Manuel to speak to him; he's got the loudest voice.'

Concha was at the door, catching up the train of her dressing gown. She was shaking her head with displeasure.

'Oh, Xavier!'

I went over to her and said:

'Are you leaving?'

'Yes, I'll come back tomorrow.'

'And tomorrow you'll do exactly the same as today.'

'No, I promise I'll come.'

She reached the bottom of the corridor and called to me in a low voice:

'Come with me; I'm terrified of spiders. But keep your voice down, that's where Isabel is sleeping.'

And her hand, which, in the shadows, was a ghost's hand, indicated a closed door which we could make out in the darkness because of the faint line of light underneath it.

'She sleeps with the light burning.'

'Yes.'

Then, stopping and pressing her head to my shoulder, I said:

'You see, Isabel can't sleep alone either. Let's follow her example.'

I picked her up in my arms as if she were a child and she laughed silently. I carried her to her bedroom door, which stood open onto the darkness, and there I set her down on the threshold.

I went to bed exhausted, and all morning my dreams were permeated by the sound of the two little girls running about, laughing and shouting on the terrace. Three of the doors of the room which I was using as a bedroom opened onto that terrace. I slept little and during that state of vague, anxious consciousness – in which I noticed whenever the girls paused outside one of the doors or called out from one of the balconies – the fat green botfly of nightmare flew round and round, like the constantly turning spindle of the spinning witches. Suddenly, it seemed to me that the children had moved off, running past my three doors. A voice was calling them from the garden. The terrace was suddenly deserted. In the middle of that torpor, which somehow painfully trammelled my will, I sensed that my thoughts were becoming lost in dark labyrinths; I heard the dull buzz of the hornet's nest that breeds evil fantasies and tormenting, capricious, distorted ideas dancing to fantastic rhythms. In the midst of the silence, the cheerful barking of dogs and the tinkle of bells rang out on the terrace. A grave, ecclesiastical voice, that seemed to come from a long way away, was calling:

'Here, Carabel! Here, Capitán!'

It was the Abbot of Brandeso, who had come over to the palace after mass to pay his respects to my noble cousin.

'Here, Carabel! Here, Capitán!'

Concha and Isabel were saying goodbye to the abbot from the terrace.

'Goodbye, Don Benicio!'

And as he went down the steps, he was saying:

'Goodbye, ladies! Go in now, there's a cold wind out here. Here, Carabel! Here, Capitán!'

I could vaguely hear the dogs frolicking about. Then, in the midst of a great silence, I heard Concha's languid voice:

'Don Benicio, don't forget that tomorrow you're celebrating mass in our chapel.'

And the grave, ecclesiastical voice replied:

'I won't forget, I won't forget.'

And it rose like a Gregorian chant from the depths of the garden amongst the tinkling of bells from the dogs. Then the two ladies said goodbye again. And the grave, ecclesiastical voice repeated:

'Here, Carabel! Here, Capitán! Tell the Marquis that I was out hunting with the chaplain a few days ago and we came across a covey of partridges. Ask him if he fancies going hunting for them sometime. Don't say anything to the chaplain though if he comes by the palace. It's our little secret.'

Concha and Isabel walked past the three doors. Their voices were a cool, gentle murmur. The terrace grew quiet again and in that silence I came completely awake. Unable to get back to sleep, I rang the silver bell, which had a noble ecclesiastical glow about it in the half-darkness of the bedroom, standing as it did on an old table covered with a crimson velvet cloth. Florisel came to help me as I dressed. Time passed, and again I heard the voices of the two little girls returning from the dovecote with Candelaria. They had brought with them a pair of doves and were talking excitedly. Candelaria was saying to them, as if recounting a fairytale, that if they clipped the birds' wings, they could let them loose in the palace.

'Your mother loved to do that when she was your age!'

Florisel opened the three doors that gave onto the terrace and I leaned out to call to the girls, who ran to kiss me, each bearing a white dove. When I saw them, I was reminded of the heavenly gifts given to the little princesses who adorn the Golden Legend like azure lilies. The girls said to me:

'Did you know that our uncle from Lantañón left at dawn on your horse?'

'Who told you?'

'We went to see him and found everything open, the doors and the windows, and the bed was all unmade. Candelaria says she saw him leave, and Florisel did too.'

I couldn't help laughing.

'Does your mother know?'

'Yes.'

'And what does she say?'

The little girls looked at each other hesitantly, exchanging smiles, then both exclaimed at once.

'Mama says he's mad.'

Candelaria called to them, and they ran off to clip the doves' wings and to let them loose in the rooms of the palace – the game that poor Concha had so loved as a child.

In the bright torpor of the afternoon, with all the windows golden in the sunshine and the doves fluttering above our heads, Isabel and the children were talking of going with me to Lantañón to find out if Don Juan Manuel had arrived safely. Isabel said:

'How far is it, Xavier?'

'No more than a league.'

'Then we can go on foot.'

'Won't the little ones get tired?'

'They're great walkers.'

And the girls, their faces shining, rushed to confirm this, both exclaiming at once:

'Last year we climbed all the way up Pico Sagro and we weren't in the least bit tired.'

Isabel looked out into the garden.

'I think we'll have good weather.'

'Who knows. Those clouds look like rain clouds.'

'But they're going in the other direction.'

Isabel trusted in the gallantry of the clouds. The two of us were sitting talking in a window seat, looking out at the sky and the fields, while the girls kept clapping and shouting to frighten the doves and make them fly. When I turned, I saw Concha. She was standing at the door, looking terribly pale, her lips trembling. She looked at me and her eyes seemed quite different – in them I saw longing, anger, supplication. Raising her two hands to her forehead, she murmured:

'Florisel said that you were out in the garden.'

'We were.'

'Are you hiding from me?'

Isabel replied with a smile:

'Yes, in order to plot against you.'

She took the two children by the hand and led them out of the room. I was left alone with poor Concha who walked about languidly before sitting down in an armchair. Then she sighed as she had on other occasions and declared that she was dying. I went over to her cheerily, and she grew indignant.

'Go on, laugh. You're quite right to leave me alone and go off with Isabel.'

I picked up one of her hands and closed my eyes, kissing her fingers which were caught in a pale, pink, perfumed beam of light.

'Don't be so cruel, Concha!'

Her eyes were full of tears and she murmured in a low, remorseful voice:

'Why do you want to leave me all alone? I know it's not your fault, it's her, she's still mad about you, she's after you.'

I dried her eyes and said:

'The only one here who's mad is you, poor Concha. But since you're so beautiful, I never want to see you cured of your madness.'

'I'm not mad.'

'Yes you are, mad about me.'

She said with mock anger:

'No, I am not!'

'Yes, you are.'

'You're so vain.'

'In that case, why do you want to have me with you?'

Concha threw her arms around my neck and kissed me, then exclaimed, laughing:

'If it makes you so vain to be loved by me, then it must be because my love is very valuable.'

'Extremely.'

Concha ran her fingers through my hair, in a slow caress:

'Let them go, Xavier. As you see, I prefer you to my own daughters.'

Like an abandoned, submissive child, I laid my head on her breast, closed my eyes and, with sad delicious longing, breathed in her perfume – the perfume of a flower whose petals are about to fall.

'I'll do whatever you want, you know that.'

Looking into my eyes and lowering her voice, Concha murmured:

'So you won't go to Lantañón, then?'

'No.'

'Do you mind?'

'No. I'm sorry for the girls, though; they were all ready to set off.'

'They can go with Isabel. The steward can go with them.'

At that moment, a sudden shower of rain beat against the windows and the trees in the garden. The clouds covered the sun, and the afternoon acquired a sad, soulful, autumnal light. María Fernanda came in, looking very upset:

'What bad luck, Xavier! It's raining!'

Then María Isabel came in.

'You'll let us go if it clears up though, won't you, Mama?'

Concha replied:

'If it clears up, yes.'

And the two girls went and sat by the window, pressing their faces to the glass, watching it rain. Heavy, black clouds were gathering above the Sierra de Céltigos, creating a watery horizon. Calling to their flocks, shepherds were hurrying along the paths, the hoods on their capes up over their heads. A rainbow arched over the garden, and the dark cypress trees and the green, damp myrtles seemed to tremble, caught in a ray of orangish light. Holding up her skirts, clattering along in her clogs, we saw the bent figure of Candelaria walking beneath a great blue umbrella, gathering roses for the altar in the chapel.

The chapel was dank, dark, echoing. Above the retable stood a coat of arms with sixteen quarters, in gules and azure, sable and vert, or and argent. It was the coat of arms given by the Catholic kings to Captain Alonso Bendaña, founder of the Brandeso dynasty, for his great achievements. A terrible tale is told about that captain in the book of genealogy of the noble titles of Galicia. They say that when he captured his enemy, the Abbot of Mos, he dressed him in a wolf-skin and set him free in the mountains, where the abbot was savaged to death by dogs. Candelaria, Concha's nursemaid, who, like all old servants, knew the histories and genealogies of the house they worked in, used to tell us the legend of Captain Alonso Bendaña, just as it was set down in the books of genealogy that no one reads any more. Candelaria also knew that two black dwarves had carried the captain's body down into hell. It was a tradition in the Brandeso family that the men should be cruel and the women pious.

I still remember the time when there was a chaplain in the palace and my Aunt Águeda, in accordance with the venerable custom, would hear mass accompanied by all her daughters, from the dais set aside for them next to the priest. The seat was covered in crimson velvet and had a high back crowned by two coats of arms, but only my Aunt Águeda, because of her age and her many ailments, had enjoyed the privilege of sitting there. Captain Alonso Bendaña was buried to the right of the altar along with other knights of his family. Next to his tomb was the statue of a warrior at prayer, and to the left was buried Doña Beatriz de Montenegro, with other ladies of different ancestry. Beside her tomb was the statue of a nun praying, wearing the white habit of the convents founded by the Knights of St James. Like a small, kingly jewel, the lamp in the sanctuary burned day and night before the carved retable. The golden branches on the evangelical vine seemed laden with fruit. The tutelary saint was the pious king who had offered myrrh to the baby Jesus, and his gold-embroidered silk tunic glittered with the devout splendour of an oriental miracle. The light from the lamp, hung on silver chains, fluttered timidly like a caged bird, as if eager to fly up and join the saint.

Concha wanted to be the one to place the vases full of roses at the feet of the king, as the offering of a pious soul. Then, accompanied by her daughters, she knelt before the altar. From the dais, I could hear only the murmur of her voice faintly reciting the Hail Mary, but when it was the children's turn to respond, I heard all the ritual words of the prayer. Concha got to her feet, kissed the rosary, and traversed the chancel crossing herself and calling her daughters to say a prayer before the tomb of the warrior, where Don Miguel Bendaña, Concha's grandfather, was also buried. He was dying when my mother took me to the palace for the first time. Don Miguel Bendaña had been a despotic, hospitable gentleman, faithful to the noble-cum-peasant tradition of his whole lineage. Straight as a lance, he never once surrendered to plebeian values – a fine and noble madness! When he died at eighty, he still had a proud, gallant soul, as well-tempered as the hilt of an ancient sword. It took him five days to die, stoutly refusing to be confessed. My mother swore that she had never seen anything like it; the gentleman was a heretic. One night, shortly after his death, I heard someone say in a low voice that Don Miguel Bendaña had once killed one of his own servants. Concha was right to pray for his soul.

The evening was slowly dying and the prayers echoed round the silent darkness of the chapel, as deep, sad and august as an echo of the Passion. As I dozed on the dais, the girls went to sit on the steps of the altar, their dresses as white as the linen altar cloth. I could just make out a shadow praying beneath the lamp in the presbytery. It was Concha. She was holding a book open in her hands and was reading, her head bent. From time to time the wind shook the curtain at one of the high windows. Then, in the already dark sky, I saw the face of the moon, pale and supernatural, like a goddess who has her altar in woods and by lakes. Concha closed the book with a sigh and again called to her daughters. I saw their white shadows walk across the chancel and assumed that they had knelt down by their mother's side. The flame in the lamp shuddered, giving out a feeble light that fell on Concha's hands still holding the open book. In the silence, I heard her reading in slow, pious tones. The girls were listening and I could just make out their loose hair on their white clothes. Concha was reading.

It was midnight. I was sitting writing when Concha, wearing a loose monastic robe, came noiselessly into the room I was using as a bedroom.

'Who are you writing to?'

'To Doña Margarita's private secretary.'

'To tell her what?'

'I'm telling her about the offering I made to the Apostle in the name of the Queen.'

There was a moment's silence. Concha, who was standing with her hands resting on my shoulders, bent over me so that her hair brushed my forehead.

'Are you writing to her secretary or to the Queen herself?'

I turned round slowly and said coldly:

'I'm writing to her secretary. Don't tell me you're jealous of the Queen as well.'

She protested warmly:

'No, no, of course I'm not!'

I sat her down on my knees and, stroking her, said:

'Doña Margarita isn't like the other Queen . . .'

'Much of what they said about the other Queen was untrue anyway. My mother always said so, and she was one of her ladies-in-waiting.'

Seeing me smile, poor Concha looked away, blushing adorably.

'You men are always determined to believe anything bad you hear about women. Besides, a Queen is always surrounded by enemies.'

Seeing that a smile still lingered on my lips, she tweaked my black moustaches with her pale fingers and exclaimed:

'You've got a very wicked tongue on you!'

She stood up, intending to leave. I caught her hand and held her back.

'Stay, Concha. Go on, stay.'

'You know I can't, Xavier.'

I said again:

'Stay.'

'No, no. I want to go to confession tomorrow. I'm afraid of offending God.'

Then, rising to my feet, I said with icy, scornful politeness:

'So, I have a rival already?'

Concha looked at me pleadingly.

'Don't torment me, Xavier.'

'I will torment you no longer. I shall leave the palace tomorrow morning.'

She burst out tearfully, angrily:

'You won't!'

And she almost tore off the white, monastic robe that she usually wore to visit me at that hour and stood there naked and trembling. I folded her in my arms.

'My poor love!'

She looked at me through her tears, distraught and pale.

'You're so cruel. Now, I won't be able to go to confession tomorrow.'

I kissed her and said by way of consolation:

'We will go to confession together the day that I leave.'

I saw the flicker of a smile in her eyes.

'If you hope to win your freedom with a promise like that, you're very much mistaken.'

'Why?'

'Because you are my prisoner here for ever.'

And she laughed, putting her arms about my neck. Her long hair came unpinned and, taking the sombre, perfumed wave of black hair in her hands, she began beating me with it. I sighed:

'Ah, the scourge of God!'

'Be quiet, you heretic!'

'Do you remember when that used to make me almost faint away with pleasure?'

'I remember *all* the mad things you said and did.'

'Whip me, Concha, whip me as if I were a holy Nazarene. Whip me till I die!'

'Be quiet, be quiet!'

She glanced away, her hands trembling as they gathered up her dark, fragrant tresses.

'You frighten me when you say such ungodly things, yes, frighten me, because it isn't you saying them: it's Satan. Even your voice is different. It's Satan's voice!'

A shudder ran through her and she closed her eyes. My arms wound lovingly about her. It seemed to me that a prayer still hovered on her lips and, as I sealed those lips with mine, I mumbled, laughing:

'Amen! Amen! Amen!'

We were silent. Then her mouth moaned beneath my mouth:

'I'm dying!'

Her body, imprisoned in my arms, trembled as if shaken by a mortal spasm. Her deathly pale head rolled back on the pillow. Her eyelids half opened and I watched as her eyes grew anguished, lightless.

'Concha! Concha!'

As if fleeing from my kisses, her pale, cold mouth curled in a cruel grimace.

'Concha! Concha!'

I sat up and cold-bloodedly, prudently removed her arms from around my neck – they were like wax. I hesitated, not knowing what to do.

'Concha! Concha!'

Somewhere in the distance, dogs were barking. I slid silently to the floor. I picked up the candle and gazed on that now lifeless face and, with tremulous fingers, I touched her brow. The cold stillness of death terrified me. No, she could no longer answer me. I thought of running away and I cautiously opened a window. I peered out into the darkness, my scalp prickling, whilst on the other side of the room, the curtains round my bed flapped and the flames guttered on the candles in the silver candelabrum. Far off, the dogs were still barking; the wind sighed in the maze like a lost soul and, like our lives, the stars above flickered on and off.

I left the window open and, making no noise, as if I feared that my footsteps might awaken pale spectres, I went over to the door which, only moments before, she had opened with hands that then had trembled with passion and that now lay stiff and still. I peered warily out into the black corridor and stepped into the darkness. Everything in the Palace seemed to be asleep. I felt my way along the wall. My steps were so light as to be almost inaudible, but in my mind they seemed to set up fearsome echoes. At the far end of the anteroom, I saw the feeble glow of the lamp that lit the image of Jesus of Nazareth day and night. His holy face, deathly pale and partly covered by his matted hair, filled me with fear, more even than Concha's mortal face. I was shaking by the time I reached her bedroom and I stood there for a moment. I had noticed a line of light on the floor on the opposite side of the corridor which marked the door of the bedroom where my cousin Isabel was sleeping. I was afraid she might suddenly appear at her door, terrified, startled by the sound of my footsteps, and that her cries would raise the alarm throughout the palace. Then I decided to go into her room and tell her everything. I tiptoed over and, from the threshold, I called softly:

'Isabel! Isabel!'

I stopped and waited. Nothing marred the silence. I took a few steps and called again:

'Isabel! Isabel!'

Again no reply. Inside the vast room, my voice faded to nothing as if frightened of itself. Isabel was asleep. In the dim light of the candle flickering in its glass jar, in the dark depths of the room, I could just make out a wooden bed. In the silence, I could hear the slow rise and fall of my cousin Isabel's regular breathing. Her body was just a soft shape beneath the damask bedcover and her hair lay like a shadowy veil across the white pillows. I called again:

'Isabel! Isabel!'

I had reached the head of the bed and my hands happened to touch her warm, bare shoulders. I felt her shudder. In a voice thick with emotion, I shouted:

'Isabel! Isabel!'

She sat up with a start.

'Don't shout, Concha might hear.'

My eyes filled with tears and, bending low, I murmured:

'Poor Concha cannot hear us now!'

A lock of my cousin Isabel's hair brushed my lips, soft, tempting. I think I kissed it. I am a saint who always loves when he is sad. Poor Concha would have forgiven me up there in Heaven. Here on Earth, she knew how weak I was. Isabel murmured passionately:

'If I thought she could, I would lock the door.'

'What door?'

'The bedroom door, idiot, my door!'

I did not wish to arouse my cousin Isabel's suspicions. It would have been so painful and so ungallant to disabuse her. Isabel was very pious and knowing that she had misunderstood my intentions would have caused her immense suffering. All the Holy Patriarchs, all the Holy Fathers, all the Holy Monks could triumph over sin more easily than I! Those lovely women who went to tempt them were not their cousins. Fate plays some very cruel jokes! When Fate smiles on me, it always does so as it did then, with the macabre leer of one of those bandy-legged dwarves who gambol about in the moonlight amongst the chimneypots on the roofs of old castles. Her voice muffled by my kisses, Isabel said:

'I'm afraid Concha might appear at any moment.'

When I heard the poor dead woman's name, a shudder of fear ran through me, but Isabel must have thought it was simply passion. She never found out why I had come to her!

When my mortal eyes saw Concha's contorted, waxen face again, when my feverish hands touched her cold hands, I was filled with such terror that I began to pray and once more I was gripped by the temptation to flee through the open window out into the dark, mysterious garden. The silent night air shook the curtains and ruffled my hair. In the pallid sky, the stars were beginning to grow faint and the candles had gradually burned down, leaving only one alight. The old cypress trees growing outside the window lightly bent their withered tops and the white moon fled amongst them like the soul of a poor, pale wretch in torment. The distant call of a cockerel broke the silence, announcing the dawn. I shivered and looked with horror at Concha's inanimate body stretched out on my bed. Then, pulling myself together, I lit all the candles in the candelabrum and placed it at the door so that it would light the corridor. I went back into the room and, still terrified, I gathered that pale ghost up into my arms, she who had so often slept with my arms about her. I left the room bearing that sad burden. At the door, one of her hands, hanging limply down, collided with the candles and knocked over the candelabrum. On the floor, the candles continued to illumine my path with a sad, sputtering light. For a moment, I stood stock-still, listening. All I could hear was the bubbling water of the fountain in the maze. I continued on. There, at the far end of the anteroom, glowed the lamp illuminating Christ and I was afraid to walk past that livid, dishevelled image. I was afraid of those dead eyes! I retraced my steps.

To reach Concha's bedroom without going through the anteroom, I had to walk round the whole Palace. I did not hesitate. I walked through room after room, along pitch-dark corridors. Sometimes, the deserted corners of certain rooms were lit by moonlight. I slipped like a shadow past that long succession of shutterless windows with their worm-eaten frames, dark, mournful windows with leaded lights. I closed my eyes whenever I walked past a mirror, so as not to see myself. Sometimes, the darkness in the rooms was so dense that I got lost in them and had to feel my way ahead, stiff and frightened, holding Concha's body in one arm, the other stretched out in front of me so as not to stumble. Her sad, loose hair got caught on one of the doors. I felt about in the darkness trying to disentangle it, but I couldn't. It just became more and more entangled. My fearful, clumsy hand was shaking with the effort and the door kept opening and closing, creaking loudly. I was horrified to see that day was already breaking. I panicked and gave a tug. I thought Concha's body would slip out of my arms. I clung desperately on to it. Beneath her taut, sombre brow, her waxen lids were beginning to open. I had to pull fiercely and tear her beloved, fragrant locks.

At last, I reached her bedroom, the door of which stood open. The darkness there was mysterious, perfumed, warm, as if it were the keeper of the gallant secret of our assignations. What a tragic secret it would have to keep now! I lay Concha's body carefully down on her bed and crept away. At the door, I hesitated, irresolute, breathing hard. I wondered if I should go back and place one last kiss on those icy lips. I resisted the temptation, with all the scrupulousness of a mystic. I was afraid there might be something sacrilegious about the melancholy overwhelming me. The warm fragrance of her bedroom awoke in me, like a torment, voluptuous, sensual memories. I longed to savour the sweet pleasures of chaste fantasy, but I could not. The holiest things often suggest the strangest of devilish fancies, even to mystics. Still today, the memory of Concha dead evokes in me a depraved and subtle sadness. It scratches at my heart like a bright-eyed, tubercular cat. My heart bleeds and writhes and, inside me, laughs the Devil who knows how to turn all sorrows into pleasures. My memories, lost glories of the soul, are like a pale, ardent music, sad and cruel, to whose strange rhythms dances the forlorn ghost of all my loves. Poor, white ghost, the worms have eaten its eyes, and tears roll from the sockets. In the midst of a youthful ring of memories, it dances, not touching the floor, floating on a wave of perfume, the perfume that Concha used on her hair and that lives on after her. Poor Concha! All she left behind of her sojourn in life was a trail of perfume. But, then, perhaps not even the whitest and most chaste of lovers has ever been anything more than a lovely, enamelled bottle filled with aphrodisiac, nuptial perfumes.

María Isabel and María Fernanda announced themselves first by beating on the door with their childish hands. Then they shouted out in cool, crystalline voices that had the charm of fountains speaking to the grasses and the birds.

'Can we come in, Xavier?'

'Come in, my dears.'

It was already late morning and they had come at Isabel's behest to ask if I had had a good night, a sweet question that stirred feelings of remorse in my heart. The little girls stood next to me at the balcony window looking out onto the garden. The wild, green branches of a fir tree scraped against the sad, mournful panes. The fir tree shivered in the mountain wind and its branches scratched at the window as if the old, shady garden were sighing with longing for the children's games to commence. A flock of pigeons was fluttering about near the maze; then out of the cold, blue sky came a hawk with broad, dark wings.

'Kill it, Xavier! Kill it!'

I fetched my gun which was lying gathering dust in a corner and hurried back to the window. The little girls were clapping and shouting:

'Kill it! Kill it!'

At that moment, the hawk dropped down on the flock of pigeons which flew off, startled. I put my rifle to my eye and when the way was clear, I fired. A few dogs in nearby farms barked a response. The hawk plummeted to earth and the little girls ran out and brought it back, carrying it by the wings. Blood was staining its breast feathers. They bore off the hawk in triumph. I called to them, suddenly filled by a new anxiety.

'Where are you going?'

They turned at the door, smiling and happy:

'Mama will get such a fright when she wakes up!'

'No, don't!'

'It'll be such a lark!'

I did not dare to stop them and I remained alone, my soul plunged in sadness. Such a bitter wait, such a timeless moment on that joyful morning all clothed in light, until, from the depths of the palace, came innocent moans, heartrending cries and terrible sobs! Faced with the cold ghost of death scything through all the dreams in my soul's garden, I felt a dumb, desperate anguish. Ah, the lovely dreams that are love's enchantment! It was a strange sadness as if evening had fallen over my life which, like a sad winter's day, had ended only to begin once again with a sunless dawn. Poor Concha was dead. That dream-flower to whom my every word had seemed beautiful was dead, that flower to whom my every gesture seemed sovereign. Would I ever find such another pale princess with sad, spellbound eyes, someone who would always think me magnificent? The thought that I might not made me weep and I wept like an ancient god at the death of the cult that once worshipped him.

WINTER SONATA

Now that I am a very old man, I find that nearly all the women for whom I once sighed with love have died. I closed the eyes of one of them, from another I received a sad letter of farewell, and the others died when they were grandmothers and had forgotten all about me. Where once I aroused great passions, now I live in the saddest, bleakest solitude of soul, and my eyes fill with tears when I comb my snow-white hair. I sigh to remember how once it was caressed by the hands of princesses. My passage through life was like a potent flowering of all the passions. My days were, one by one, warmed by the great bonfire of love. The purest of souls once gave me their tenderness and bemoaned my cruelty and my deceptions, whilst their pale, ardent fingers pulled the petals from the daisies that guard the secrets of every heart. In order to guard one secret for all eternity, a secret that I trembled to discover, death sought out a young girl whom I will mourn for all my old age. My hair was already white when I inspired that fateful love.

I had just reached Estella, where the King had his Court. I was weary with my long peregrination about the world. I was beginning to feel something previously unknown in my bright, adventurous life, hitherto full of dangers and vicissitudes, like the life of one of those younger sons of noble families who would join the infantry in Italy in search of love, duels and fortune. I felt a fading of all my hopes, a profound sense of disillusionment with everything. It was the first chill of old age, sadder than that of death itself. When it arrived, I was still wearing about my shoulders the cloak of Almaviva and, on my head, the helmet of Mambrino. The hour had come when the ardours of the blood burn out, and when the passions of love, pride and anger – the noble, sacred passions that stirred the old gods – become the slaves of reason. I was in the declining years of my life, an age conducive to ambition and stronger than youth itself, when one has renounced the love of women. Ah, if only I had done just that!

I arrived at the Court in Estella a fugitive, wearing the habit left hanging in a farm kitchen by a contemplative monk who had decided to throw in his lot with Don Carlos VII. The bells of San Juan were ringing to announce the King's mass which, out of gratitude for having escaped with my life, I wanted to hear with the dust of the road still on me. I went into the church when the priest was already at the altar. The flickering light from a lamp illumined the chancel steps where the King's entourage were gathered. Amongst those dark forms, shapeless and faceless, my eyes could distinguish only the figure of His Majesty, who stood out in their midst with all the admirable elegance and nobility of a King in olden times. The arrogance and brio of his person seemed to call out for a lavish suit of armour created by a Milanese goldsmith, and, as a warhorse, a palfrey hung with chain mail. His bright, eagle eye would have flashed magnificently forth from beneath the visor of a helmet adorned with a crested crown and a long lambrequin. Don Carlos de Borbón y de Este is the only sovereign prince worthy to wear the ermine cloak, hold the golden sceptre and don the jewelled crown by which Kings are represented in the old codices.

Once the mass was over, a friar entered the pulpit and preached the holy war in the Basque language to the Basque troops who, having just arrived, were escorting the King for the first time. I felt very moved. Those strong, harsh words, as rough-hewn as stone-age weapons, made an indefinable impression on me. They had an ancient sonority, they were as primitive and august as the furrows made in the ground to receive the grains of wheat and corn scattered in them. Though I did not understand what was said, I felt those words to be loyal, true, austere, rugged. Don Carlos listened standing up, surrounded by his retinue, his face turned to the friar. Doña Margarita and her ladies remained kneeling. Only then was I able to recognise a few faces. That morning,

I remember, the retinue consisted of the Princes of Caserta, Marshal Valdespina, Countess María Antonieta Volfani (Doña Margarita's lady-in-waiting), the Marquis of Lantana (a nobleman from Italy), Valatié (a French legitimist), Brigadier Adelantado, and my uncle, Don Juan Manuel Montenegro.

Afraid that I might be recognised, I remained kneeling in the shadow of a pillar, until the King and Queen had left the church after the friar's sermon. Next to Doña Margarita walked a fine figure of a woman, wearing a black veil so long that it almost dragged on the floor behind her. She passed quite close and, although I could not see her face clearly, I sensed that she was looking at me and and that she recognised me in my monk's disguise. For a moment, I thought I knew who that woman was, but the memory fled before I could grasp it. It came and went like a gust of wind, like the lights that flicker on and off throughout the night along the streets. When the church was empty, I went to the sacristy. Beneath a tenuous ray of sunlight, two old priests were standing talking in a corner, and an equally ancient sacristan was standing by a tall, barred window, blowing on the embers of the censer. I paused at the door. The priests took no notice of me, but the sacristan, fixing me with smoke-reddened eyes, asked me severely:

'Has the reverend father come to say mass?'

'I have come in search of my friend, Brother Ambrosio Alarcón.'

'Brother Ambrosio will be some time.'

One of the priests intervened calmly:

'If you're in a hurry to see him, you'll doubtless find him walking outside somewhere, in the lee of the church.'

At that moment, someone knocked at the door and the sacristan went over to draw the bolt. The other priest, who until then had kept silent, murmured:

'That may be him already.'

The sacristan opened the door to reveal the figure of that famous friar, who every day of his life said a mass for the soul of Zumalacárregui. He was a hunched giant, all parchment skin and bone, with deep-set eyes and a constantly nodding head, the result of a blow to the neck that he had received as a soldier in the first Carlist war. Before he came in, the sacristan warned him in a low voice:

'There's a priest here looking for you. He must be from Rome.'

I waited. Brother Ambrosio looked me up and down without recognising me, but that did not stop him placing one frank and friendly hand on my shoulder:

'Are you quite sure it's Brother Ambrosio Alarcón you want to talk to?'

I made no reply; I simply pushed back the hood of my cloak. The old soldier looked at me with happy surprise. Then, turning to the other priests, he exclaimed:

'This reverend father is known to the world as the Marquis of Bradomín.'

The sacristan stopped blowing on the embers in the censer, and the two priests sitting by the brazier beneath the ray of sun stood up, smiling beatifically. I enjoyed a moment's vanity at their welcome which demonstrated what a famous figure I was in the court of Estella. They looked at me with love and just a touch of fatherly disapproval. They were, after all, men of the cloth, and perhaps recalled some of my more worldly adventures.

They all crowded round me. I had to tell them the story behind my monk's habit and how I had crossed the frontier. Brother Ambrosio laughed jovially, while the priests peered at me over their spectacles, a look of uncertainty on their toothless mouths. Behind them, beneath the ray of sun coming in through a narrow window, the sacristan stood absolutely still, listening, and whenever Brother Ambrosio interrupted me, he would scold him:

'Let him finish telling his story, man!'

But Brother Ambrosio was reluctant to believe that I had just left a monastery where I had sought refuge, disillusioned with the world and repenting of my many sins. More than once, while I was talking, he would turn to the other priests, muttering:

'Don't believe him; it's just one of our illustrious Marquis' amusing inventions.'

To put paid to his doubts, I had to swear a solemn oath. From that point on, he affected a look of profound belief, constantly crossing himself in amazement.

'People are quite right when they say that you live and learn. I would never have thought of the Marquis as an infidel exactly, but I would certainly never have imagined this religious side to his nature.'

I murmured gravely:

'Repentance does not arrive like the cavalry, with bugles blowing.'

At that moment, the bugle call for saddling up sounded and everyone laughed. Then one of the priests asked me in kindly, foolish tones:

'I imagine that repentance did not arrive as slyly as the serpent either?'

I gave a melancholy sigh.

'It arrived when I looked at myself in the mirror and saw my white hair.'

The two priests exchanged such a cautious smile that I immediately took them for Jesuits. I adopted a penitent pose, my hands folded over my scapular, and sighed:

'Now my ill fortune has tossed me back into the sea of the world. I managed to conquer every passion but that of pride. Despite this rough habit I could not forget that I am a Marquis.'

Brother Ambrosio raised his arms and said in a grave voice that seemed made for telling convent jokes:

'Even the Emperor Charles V could not forget his empire when he was in the monastery of Yuste.'

The two priests again smiled their catechistic smiles and, from where he sat in the ray of sun coming in through the narrow window, the sacristan grumbled:

'Why can't you just let him tell his story?'

Having spoken, Brother Ambrosio laughed long and loud, and the dark, formless echo of that jovial laughter still lingered in the vault of the sacristy when a pale seminarian entered, his mouth as red as any virgin's, in contrast to his white, aquiline profile, with its hooked nose and round, heavy-lidded eyes, which gave his face a cruel expression. Brother Ambrosio received him, bowing from the waist, laughing so hard that his trembling head seemed about to fall from his shoulders.

'Welcome, sublime and as yet undiscovered captain! A new Epaminondas whose deeds, with the passing of the centuries, will be set down by another Cornelius Nepos. Come in and meet the Marquis of Bradomín!'

The seminarian greeted me, blushing scarlet and removing the black beret which, together with an already threadbare cassock, completed the attire of this elegant personage. Brother Ambrosio placed a hand on his shoulder and shook him with rough affection, saying:

'If this young man can gather together fifty men, then we'll set those tongues wagging. He's another Don Ramón Cabrera – he's as brave as a lion!'

The seminarian stepped back to free himself from the hand still weighing on his shoulder and then, fixing me with his birdlike eyes, he said, as if in answer to my thoughts:

'Some people believe that to be a great captain, you don't need to be brave, and maybe they're right. Who knows, had Don Ramón Cabrera been a little less bold his military genius might have proved more fertile.'

Brother Ambrosio looked at him scornfully.

'Epaminondas, my son, with a little less boldness, he might have ended up saying mass, which could well be what happens to you.'

The seminarian gave an admirable smile.

'That definitely won't happen to me, Brother Ambrosio.'

The two priests sitting by the brazier said nothing, they merely smiled. One was stretching out trembling hands to the blaze, the other was leafing through his breviary, and the sacristan was half-closing his eyes ready to follow the example of the cat dozing on his lap. Brother Ambrosio instinctively lowered his voice:

'You say these things because you're a boy, and you believe in the cunning arguments by which certain generals, who would have been better off as bishops, excuse their fear. I've seen a lot of things. I was a monk in a monastery in Galicia when the first war broke out, and I hung up my habit and fought for seven years in the King's army. And I can tell you that to be a great captain, you must first be a great soldier. Take no notice of people who say that Napoleon was a coward.'

The seminarian's eyes shone like the sun glinting on the blue-black steel of two bullets:

'Brother Ambrosio, if I had a hundred men, I would lead them like a soldier, but if I had a thousand, only a thousand, then I would lead them like a captain. For then I could guarantee the triumph of the cause. We do not need large armies in this war; with a thousand men I would lead an expedition throughout the whole kingdom, as did the greatest of the generals in the last war, Don Miguel Gómez, thirty-five years ago.'

Brother Ambrosio interrupted him and said in a bossy, scornful, though still playful voice:

'Illustrious, beardless warrior, have you ever heard tell of a certain Don Tomás Zumalacárregui? *He* was the greatest general of the cause. If we had a man like him today, then our success would be assured.'

The seminarian said nothing, but the two priests seemed almost scandalised. One said:

'We cannot doubt the success of the cause.'

And the other:

'The justice of our cause is the best general we have.'

Beneath my penitent's habit I felt a rekindling of that fire that filled St Bernard when he preached in favour of the crusades, and I said:

'The best general is the help of our Lord God!'

There was a murmur of approval, impassioned as any prayer. The seminarian smiled to himself but still said nothing. Meanwhile, the bells tolled gravely and the old sacristan got to his feet, pushing the sleeping cat off his lap. A few priests arrived, come to sing at a funeral. The seminarian donned his surplice and the sacristan handed him the censer. The aromatic smoke filled the vast room. You could hear the sombre murmur of hoarse, ecclesiastical voices as the priests donned their linen albs, their surplices especially ironed by the nuns, and the golden chasubles still redolent of myrrh burned a hundred years before. The seminarian went into the church, clinking the chains of the censer, and the priests, fully dressed now, followed behind. I remained alone with Brother Ambrosio, who opened wide his great arms and pressed me to his breast, saying in a low, emotional voice:

'Does the Marquis still remember when I taught him Latin at the monastery in Sobrado?'

And then, after the introit of a cough, and recovering his old theologian's smile, he purred as if in the confessional box:

'The illustrious hero will forgive me if I say that I did not believe one word of the story with which you regaled us a moment ago.'

'What story?'

'The story about your conversion. May one know the truth?'

'When no one can hear us, Brother Ambrosio.'

He nodded gravely. I fell silent, pitying that poor ex-monk who preferred history to legend and was curious to know the details of a far less interesting, less exemplary and less beautiful story than the one I had invented. Ah, jovial, wingèd lie, when will men finally be persuaded that it must be allowed to triumph. When will they learn that those souls in which only the light of truth exists are sad, tormented, austere souls who converse with death in the silence and spread over life a pall of ashes? Hail to thee, bright lie, bird of light that sings like hope itself. And you, parched Thebaids, historic cities full of sunshine and silence, perishing beneath the voice of the bells, do not let it slip away, like so many other things, through the crumbling city walls! It is to be found in flirtatious talk at a barred window, in the lustre on worm-eaten coats of arms, in the mirrors in the muddy river flowing beneath the Roman arches of bridges. Like confession, it comforts grieving hearts, makes them flower, restores them to grace. Take note that this too is a gift from heaven. Thus, ancient race of the sun and of the bull, may you preserve for all eternity your mendacious, hyperbolic, blustering genius, and thus will you for ever be lulled to sleep by the strumming of guitars, with all your griefs consoled, though the Indies be lost and gone, like those convent meals once given to the poor. Amen!

Brother Ambrosio considered it his honourable duty to find shelter for me, and I had to submit to his hospitality. We left the church together and walked through the streets of the loyal city, the holy ark of the cause. It had snowed and, in the shelter of the sombre houses, the snow had left behind it an immaculate wake. The rain dripped from the blackened eaves; leaning out from one of the narrow windows beneath them, we occasionally saw the figure of an old woman, a scarf tied about her head, peering out into the street to see if the weather had cleared up enough for her to go to mass. We passed by a big, old house surrounded by walls so high that one could see only the tops of the cypresses in the garden; we saw an ostentatious coat of arms, rusted railings and a studded door which stood ajar to reveal, in the half-light, a hallway with gleaming steps and a great iron lantern. Brother Ambrosio said to me:

'That is the house of the Duchess of Uclés.'

I smiled, guessing the monk's cunning intention.

'Is she still as beautiful as she used to be?'

'So they say, though I couldn't actually tell you, since she always wears a veil.'

I could not suppress a sigh.

'She was once a great friend of mine.'

The monk coughed sarcastically:

'So I hear.'

'A secret of the confessional?'

'An open secret. A lowly ex-monk like myself does not have such illustrious spiritual daughters.'

We continued on in silence. I could not help but remember better times, the days when I was a handsome young man and a poet. Those far-off days bloomed in my memory with all the charm of an almost forgotten tale that brings with it the perfume of faded roses and the old harmonies of poetry. Ah, they were the roses and the poetry of the good old days, when my beautiful friend was still a dancer – brief oriental prayers written in her honour, describing her lithe body as a palm tree in the desert, and declaring that all the Graces gathered about her skirts singing and laughing to the sound of golden bells. Her beauty was indeed beyond all praise. Her name was Carmen and she was as sweet as that name is full of Andalusian wit and grace, for in Latin it means poetry and in Arabic a garden. When I remembered her, I remembered too all the years that had passed without my seeing her and how the monk's habit I was wearing would once have provoked her into crystalline laughter. Almost without thinking, I said to Brother Ambrosio:

'Does the duchess still live in Estella?'

'She is lady-in-waiting to Queen Margarita, but she never leaves the palace except to hear mass.'

'I'm tempted to turn round and go in to see her.'

'There's time enough for that.'

We had reached Santa María and had to stand in the doorway of the church to allow a troop of soldiers on horseback to pass. They were Castilian lancers returning from duty outside the city. The warm chorus of bugles mingled with loud neighing, and the valiant, martial sound of hooves rang out on the old cobbled streets, the same sound as described in ballads when they speak of the paladins. The cavalry passed by and we continued on our way. Brother Ambrosio said to me:

'Nearly there.'

He pointed to the bottom of the street, at a small house with a worm-eaten wooden balcony supported by columns. An old greyhound was sleeping by the doorway; it growled when it saw us but did not get up. The hallway was dark and smelled of hay and the breath of cattle. We groped our way up stairs that trembled beneath our feet. When we got to the top, the monk pulled hard on a chain hanging by the door and, somewhere inside, a clucking bell danced and clattered. We heard footsteps and the voice of the housekeeper grumbling:

'What a way to call at a house! What do you want?'

The monk replied imperiously:

'Open up!'

'Holy Mother of God, what's the hurry!'

The woman was still grumbling as she drew the bolt. The monk in turn muttered impatiently:

'The woman's unbearable.'

Once we were through the door, the housekeeper grew still angrier:

'I see you've got company again. Of course there's always so much food in the house that you just have to bring someone back with you to help finish it up.'

White with rage, Brother Ambrosio raised his huge, thin, threatening arms. His ancient parchment hands danced above his ever-bobbing head.

'Silence that scorpion tongue of yours! Be silent and have a little respect. Do you know who you have offended with your insults? Do you? Do you know who you have before you? Ask the Marquis of Bradomín's pardon, now.'

Ah, the insolence of the concubine! When she heard my name, the hag showed neither repentance nor unease. She fixed her black witch's eyes on me – the kind of eyes you see in some of Goya's paintings of old women – and, looking slightly incredulous, she merely muttered out of the corner of her mouth:

'If he is the gentleman you say he is, may he be so for many more years. Amen.'

She stood to one side to let us pass. We could still hear her muttering:

'Just look at the mud they've got on their feet. Holy Jesus, look at the mess they've made of my floors.'

Those clean, waxed, shining floors, pure mirrors in which she could see her own face, the pride and joy of an old housekeeper, had just been barbarously profaned by our feet. I turned round anxiously to take in the full horror of my sacrilege, and such was the look of hatred in the old woman's eyes that I felt afraid. She was still grumbling:

'You'd think they'd been out slaughtering incendiaries. Look at the state they've left my floors in! The cheek of it!'

Brother Ambrosio shouted from the living room:

'Be quiet and bring us some hot chocolate – now!'

And his voice rang through the silent house like a war-like report. It was a voice that once held sway over the men in his troop — the only voice that would make them tremble — but that old woman clearly belonged to the other side, for she merely averted her pasty face and muttered more sourly than ever:

'You'll get it when it's ready. Dear God, give me patience.'

Brother Ambrosio gave a cavernous cough and in the depths of the house we could hear the muffled mutterings of his concubine, then, when silence was restored, the ticking of a clock, as if it were the pulse of that monk's house ruled over by an old woman and her menage of cats. Tick tock tick tock. It was a wall clock with a pendulum and weights. The monk's cough, the old woman's grumblings and the clock's soliloquy seemed to me to keep a bizarre, grotesque rhythm, learned on the clavichord of some music-loving witch.

I took off my monk's habit and stood there in the zouave uniform of a papal guard. Brother Ambrosio looked at me with childish delight, waving his long, stiff arms about:

'That's a strange get-up!'

'Haven't you seen it before?'

'Only in paintings, in a portrait of the Infante Don Alfonso.'

And, eager to learn of my adventures, he said in a low voice, his tonsured head trembling on his shoulders:

'So, are you going to tell me the story behind that monk's habit?'

I said coolly:

'It was a disguise I needed in order to avoid falling into the hands of that wretched priest.'

'Santa Cruz?'

'Yes.'

'He's set up camp in Oyarzun now.'

'And I've just come from Arimendi where I was so badly stricken with fever that I had to hide on a farm.'

'Good grief! And why is Santa Cruz after your blood?'

'He knows that I got the King to sign the order for Lizárraga to shoot him.'

'Not a good idea, not a good idea at all.'

I replied imperiously:

'He's no better than a bandit.'

'Such bandits are necessary in wartime, except, of course, that this isn't a war, it's just a masonic farce!'

I had to smile.

'Masonic?'

'Yes, masonic. Dorregaray is a mason.'

'But Lizárraga is the one who wants to hunt the dog down, the one who has sworn to exterminate him.'

The monk turned towards me, clutching his trembling head with both hands, as if he were afraid it might roll from his shoulders.

106

'Don Antonio believes that the war can be won by spilling a few drops of holy water, not blood. Everything can be sorted out with a few communion services, but in war, if you take communion, it has to be with lead bullets. Don Antonio is just a wretched old monk like me, or rather, much more so than me; he was even before he took his vows. We old men who took part in the first war, we look at this one and we feel utterly ashamed. Now it's given me the palsy.'

He gripped his head harder and sat down in the armchair to wait for the hot chocolate, for we could already hear the old woman's footsteps in the corridor and the clink of cups on metal trays. She came in wearing a completely changed expression, her face now the placid, smiling face of old ladies who live contented lives, doing their household chores and their knitting, and saying the rosary.

'What a happy day this is for us. The Marquis won't remember me, but I once bounced him on my knee. I'm the sister of Micaela la Galana. Do you remember Micaela la Galana? She was a maid who for many years served your grandmother, my mistress, the countess.'

I looked at the old woman, quite touched, and said:

'I'm afraid, Señora, that I barely remember my grandmother.'

'She was a saint that woman. She'll be sitting now in Heaven on our Lord Jesus' right hand.'

She set the two trays with the hot chocolate on them down on the table, and, after whispering something in the monk's ear, she withdrew. The hot chocolate smelled exquisite. It was the traditional hot chocolate, flavoured with vanilla and other spices, that used to be drunk in convents and which, in the olden days, was sent as a gift to abbots by the viceroys of the Indies. My old grammar teacher could still remember those fortunate times. Ah, the cosy comforts, the ecclesiastical opulence, the joyous gluttony – so sorely missed – of the royal and imperial monastery of Sobrado. True to tradition, Brother Ambrosio mumbled a few prayers before raising the cup to his lips. When he had finished it, he said, as if passing sentence with all the elegant concision of one of the classic writers of Augustus' time.

'Delicious! No one makes hot chocolate like those wonderful Santa Clara nuns!'

He sighed contentedly and returned to the story I had been telling.

'It was just as well that you didn't tell the true story behind your disguise in the sacristy. The priests there are all loyal supporters of Santa Cruz.'

He sat for a moment, thinking. Then he gave a long yawn and made the sign of the cross over his gaping, black mouth, like the mouth of a wolf.

'And what does the Marquis of Bradomín want from this poor ex-monk?'

With feigned indifference, I said:

'We can talk about that later.'

The monk murmured slyly:

'That might not be necessary ... because, as it happens, I still work as chaplain in the house of the Countess of Volfani. The countess is well, although a little sad perhaps. As it happens, this is exactly the right time to visit her.'

I made a vague gesture, and took a gold coin from my purse.

'Let us forget about worldly business, Brother Ambrosio. This is for a mass to give thanks for my safe escape.'

The monk silently pocketed it, and went on to offer me his bed on which to take a nap and recover from my journey. It was a bed with seven mattresses on it and a crucifix at the head. Opposite was a large pot-bellied chest of drawers with a horn inkwell on top, and perched on the inkwell a cardinal's cap.

It rained all day. In the brief moments when the rain let up, a sad, grey light dawned on the mountains surrounding the holy Carlist city, where the sound of rain on windows is a familiar one. From time to time, in the midst of that afternoon of winter tedium, there came the urgent sound of bugles or the ringing of bells by nuns calling people to the novena. I had to present myself to the King and I left the house before Brother Ambrosio got back. A veil of mist drifted on the gusting wind. Two soldiers were walking wearily across the square, their capes dripping. You could hear the monotonous chanting of children in school. The pale afternoon made the vacant space of the gloomy, flooded, deserted square seem even sadder. I got lost several times in the streets, for the only person I came across to ask directions was a woman on her way to church. It was already dark when I reached the King's house.

'You soon hung up your habit, Bradomín.'

Those were the words with which Don Carlos greeted me. I replied, hoping that only the King would hear me:

'I kept tripping over them, sir.'

The King replied in a similar vein:

'The same thing happens to me, but I, alas, cannot hang mine up.'

I ventured a reply:

'Well, sir, if you cannot hang them, you should have them shot.'

The King smiled and led me to a window seat:

'I know you've spoken to Cabrera. These are his ideas. Cabrera, as you will have seen, is the declared enemy of the ultramontane party and of all troublesome priests. He is wrong to take that position, because now they offer us some powerful support. Believe me, without them the war would not be possible.'

'Sir, as you know, the General is also against the war.'

The King fell silent for a moment.

'I know. Cabrera thinks that it would have been more productive to continue the underground work of the Juntas. I believe he is wrong. For the rest, I myself am no friend of troublesome priests. I told you as much on another occasion, when you advised me to have Santa Cruz shot. The reason why I was, for some time, opposed to forming a council of war, was to prevent the republican troops engaged in pursuing him from getting together and coming down on top of us. As you see, that is precisely what happened. That priest has now cost us the loss of Tolosa.'

The King paused again and looked about the room, a dark room with a walnut floor, the walls hung with weapons and with flags won in the seven-year war by those old generals of now legendary memory. At the far end, the Bishop of Urgel, Carlos Calderón and Diego Villadarias were talking in low voices. The King smiled faintly, a smile of sad indulgence, that I had never before seen on his face.

'They're jealous because I am talking to you, Bradomín. You are certainly not one of the Bishop's favourite people.'

'Why do you say that, sir?'

'Because of the way he's looking at you. Go and kiss his ring.'

I was just about to obey that order, when the King, in a loud voice so that everyone could hear him, said:

'Bradomín, don't forget that you will be dining with me tonight.'

I gave a deep bow:

'Thank you, sir.'

And I went over to join the Bishop's group, who fell silent at my approach. His Grace received me with cool kindness:

'Welcome, Marquis.'

I replied with lordly condescension, as if the Bishop of Urgel were merely a chaplain in my house.

'Delighted to see you, Your Grace.'

And with a bow more courtly than pious, I kissed the pastoral amethyst. His Grace, who had the proud spirit of those feudal bishops who used to wear their weapons beneath their cope, frowned and ventured a castigating homily.

'Marquis, I have just uncovered a crude plot hatched this morning to make fools of two innocent, credulous priests, at the same time making a mockery of the cloth, and showing absolutely no respect for the sanctity of the place, for it happened in San Juan, and . . .'

I broke in:

'In the sacristy, Your Grace.'

His Grace, who was somewhat out of breath, paused and said:

'They told me it happened in the church, but even if it did take place in the sacristy, Marquis, the story still makes mock of the lives of certain saints. If, as I imagine, the habit was not some carnival disguise, then there was no profanity in it, but the story you told to the priests was worthy of that heathen Voltaire.'

The prelate was doubtless about to launch into an attack on the authors of the *Encyclopédie* and, seeing that, I said in a voice of tremulous repentance:

'I acknowledge my guilt in the matter and am prepared to carry out whatever penance Your Grace sees fit to impose on me.'

Taking this as evidence of the triumph of his eloquence, the saintly gentleman smiled benevolently.

'We will do our penance together.'

I looked at him uncomprehendingly. Resting one white, dimpled hand on my shoulder, he clarified his ironic remark:

'We shall both dine at the King's table, where fasting is unavoidable. Don Carlos has the sober habits of a soldier.'

I replied:

'The dream of his grandfather was that each of his subjects should be able to afford to sacrifice a chicken. Recognising that dream as a poetic fancy, Don Carlos prefers to fast along with all his vassals.'

The bishop interrupted me.

'That's enough joking, Marquis. The King too is sacred.'

I placed my right hand on my breast, indicating that even had I wanted to forget that fact I could not, for his altar was there in my heart. Then I took my leave, for I had to pay my respects to Doña Margarita.

When I went into the antechamber, where the Queen and her ladies were busy embroidering scapulars for the soldiers, I experienced an emotion which was at once religious and gallant. I understood then the ingenuous sentiments that fill novels of chivalry, as well as that cult of female beauty and tears that makes Tirant lo Blanc's heart beat faster beneath his doublet. More than ever, I felt that I was a knight of the cause. I wanted to die for that lady with hands like lilies and a name perfumed with legend, the name of some pale, saintly, long-ago princess. Doña Margarita inspired a loyalty that belonged to another age. She received me with a gracious, melancholy smile.

'Don't be offended if I carry on embroidering this scapular, Bradomín. I receive you as I would a friend.'

And leaving her needle impaled in the embroidery for a moment, she held out her hand, which I kissed respectfully. The Queen went on:

'They tell me you've been ill. You do seem a little pale. You look like the kind of man who doesn't take enough care of himself and that's not good at all. If you won't do it for yourself, then do it for the King, who is in desperate need of loyal servants like yourself. We are surrounded by traitors, Bradomín.'

Doña Margarita fell silent for a moment. When she said those last words, her silvery voice shook slightly, and I thought she might break down and weep. I may have imagined it, but it seemed to me that her eyes, beautiful and chaste as the eyes of a Madonna, were full of tears. I cannot be sure, though, for she immediately bent her head over her embroidery again. Some time passed. The Queen sighed and looked up. She wore her hair parted in the middle, and her brow had about it a lunar whiteness.

'Bradomín, it is up to loyal men like yourself to save the King.'

Moved, I replied:

'Madam, I am ready to give every last drop of my blood in order that he might wear the crown.'

The Queen looked at me loftily.

'You have misunderstood me. It is not his crown I am asking you to defend, it is his life. Do not let it be said of the knights of Spain that you went off to distant lands in search of a princess only to dress her in mourning. I say to you again, Bradomín, we are surrounded by traitors.'

The Queen fell silent again. You could hear the sound of the rain on the windows and the distant blowing of bugles. There were three ladies-in-waiting present: Doña Juana Pacheco, Doña Manuela Ozores and María Antonieta Volfani. From the moment I entered the room I had felt the latter's eyes on me, like a loving magnet. Taking advantage of the silence that had fallen, she got up and walked over to Doña Margarita.

'Shall I go and fetch the prince and princess, my lady?'

The Queen in turn asked:

'Will they have finished their lessons?'

'They will.'

'Go and get them then. Bradomín can meet them.'

I bowed and took the opportunity to greet María Antonieta as well. Showing the most perfect self-control, she responded with some insignificant words that I no longer remember, but the look in her dark, ardent eyes was such that it made my heart beat as it used to when I was twenty. She went out and the Queen said:

'I'm concerned about María Antonieta. For some time now she has seemed very sad and I'm afraid she may be suffering from the same illness as her sisters, both of whom died of tuberculosis, and then, of course, the poor thing is so very unhappy with her husband.'

She stuck her needle in the red damask pincushion in her silver workbasket and, smiling, showed me the scapular she had made.

'There you are. A present for you, Bradomín.'

I went over to receive it from her royal hands, and the Queen gave it to me, saying:

'May it protect you from enemy bullets!'

Doña Juana Pacheco and Doña Manuela Ozores, venerable old ladies who could remember the seven-year war, murmured:

'Amen.'

There was another silence. Suddenly, the Queen's eyes lit up with loving joy: her two eldest children had just come in, led by María Antonieta. They ran to her from the door, and hung about her neck and kissed her. Doña Margarita said to them with mock severity:

'Who has learned their lessons best then?'

The Infanta blushed scarlet and said nothing, while Don Jaime, who was the bolder of the two, replied:

'Both of us.'

'That means neither of you did.'

And Doña Margarita kissed them to hide her laughter. Then, gesturing towards me with one delicate, white hand, she said:

'This gentleman is the Marquis of Bradomín.'

Resting her head on her mother's shoulder, the Infanta murmured:

'The one who went to war in Mexico?'

The Queen stroked her daughter's hair.

'Who told you that?'

'Didn't María Antonieta tell us?'

'What a memory you have!'

The little girl came over to me, her eyes full of shy curiosity.

'Marquis, did you wear that uniform in Mexico?'

From his mother's side, Don Jaime said loudly, with all the authority of an eldest child:

'Don't be so silly! You're useless at uniforms. That one's from the papal guard, just like Uncle Alfonso's.'

With a mixture of familiarity and courtesy, the prince joined us.

'Marquis, is it true that in Mexico the horses can gallop all day and never get tired?'

'It is, Your Highness.'

The Infanta asked in turn:

'And is it true that they have serpents there called glass snakes?'

'That's true too, Your Highness.'

The children reflected for a moment, then their mother said to them:

'Tell Bradomín what you're studying.'

Hearing this, the prince, with childish arrogance, pulled himself up very straight and said:

'Marquis, ask me anything you like about the history of Spain.'

I smiled.

'How many Kings have borne your name, Your Highness?'

'Only one. Don Jaime the Conqueror.'

'And what was he the King of?'

'Of Spain.'

The Infanta, again blushing scarlet, murmured:

'It was Aragon, wasn't it, Marquis?'

'That's right, Your Highness.'

The prince looked at her scornfully.

'Well, that's Spain, isn't it?'

The Infanta looked to me for encouragement and said with shy gravity:

'But not the whole of Spain.'

She blushed again. She was a delightful child, with lively eyes and long ringlets that brushed the velvet skin of her cheeks. Plucking up her courage, she asked me more about my travels:

'Marquis, is it true that you've been to the Holy Land too?'

'I have, Your Highness.'

'And did you see our Lord's tomb? Tell me what it's like.'

And she sat down on a stool to listen, her elbows on her knees and her face cupped in her hands, almost lost beneath her long hair. Doña Manuela Ozores and Doña Juana Pacheco, who were engaged in a whispered conversation, fell silent too, keen to hear the story. At that point, however, the time to do penance arrived — at the royal altar of the King's table, exactly as His Grace had prophesied.

I had the honour of attending the Queen's soirée and, while I was there, I sought in vain a propitious moment to speak to María Antonieta alone. I left with a vague feeling that she had been avoiding me all night. When the cold of the street hit my face, I noticed a tall, almost gigantic shadow coming towards me. It was Brother Ambrosio.

'The King and Queen have treated you very well. You certainly have no reason for complaint, Marquis.'

I replied in a rather surly tone:

'The King knows that he has no more loyal servant than me.'

And he said in an equally surly manner, but in a quieter tone of voice:

'There must be some.'

I felt my pride swell.

'None!'

We walked in silence until we came to a corner by a lamp post. There Brother Ambrosio stopped. I asked him:

'But where are we going?'

'The lady in question says that, if you wish, she will see you this very night.'

I felt my heart beat faster.

'Where?'

'At her house. It will be necessary to use great stealth. I will guide you.'

We retraced our steps, walking back down the wet, deserted street. Brother Ambrosio spoke to me in a low voice:

'The countess has herself only just left the Queen's soirée. This morning she sent orders for me to wait for her. She doubtless wanted me to give you this message. She was afraid she might not be able to speak to you at the King's house.'

He stopped talking then and sighed, before uttering a strange, loud, grotesque laugh.

'Great God!'

'What's wrong, Brother Ambrosio?'

'Nothing, Marquis. I'm just so thrilled to find myself carrying out such tasks, so very worthy of an old warrior. Ah, how my seventeen scars are laughing.'

'You're keeping track of them, are you?'

'I've got the receipts too.'

He fell silent again, doubtless waiting for some response from me, and when he did not get it, he continued in the same tone of bitter mockery.

'There's no privilege like being chaplain to the Countess of Volfani. It's a shame she isn't better at keeping her promises. She says that it's not her fault, that it's the fault of the royal household. They are against interfering priests, and she cannot risk displeasing them. Ah, if it all depended on my protectress . . .'

I stopped him and spoke to him firmly:

'Enough, Brother Ambrosio, my patience has run out. I won't listen to another word.'

He bowed his head.

'Fine.'

We walked on, not speaking. From time to time we passed a street lamp, and all around it the shadows danced. When we walked past the houses where troops were billeted, we heard the thrum of guitars and strong, young voices singing. Then silence returned, broken only by the shouts of sentinels and the barking of dogs. We walked beneath a colonnade and kept cautiously in the shadows. Brother Ambrosio went ahead, showing me the way. A door opened quietly. He turned, gesturing to me to follow and disappeared into the hall. I went after him and heard him say:

'Is it all right to light a candle?'

And another voice, a woman's voice, replied in the darkness:

'Yes, sir.'

The door had closed again. I waited, lost in the darkness, while Brother Ambrosio lit a wax taper that burned, giving off a smell of churches. The pale flame trembled in the broad hallway, and that flickering light lit his own tremulous head. A shadow approached. It was María Antonieta's maid. Brother Ambrosio handed her the light and led me to a corner. I could sense, though not see, the violent trembling of that tonsured head.

'Marquis, I'm going to abandon this job as go-between – so unworthy of me.'

And a skeletal hand gripped my shoulder.

'The moment has come to enjoy the fruits of my labours, Marquis. You must give me a hundred gold coins. If you haven't got them on you, you can ask the Countess for them. After all, it was she who offered them to me.'

I was not frightened, although I was surprised, and, stepping back, I put my hand on my sword.

'You have chosen the worst possible way of going about things. No one threatens me or tries to frighten me with brave gestures, Brother Ambrosio.'

He gave that grotesquely mocking laugh again.

'Don't raise your voice, a passing patrol might hear us.'

'Are you afraid?'

'I've never been afraid. But what if it were a married woman's entourage . . .'

Realising his mischievous intentions, I said to him, my voice restrained, hoarse:

'This is some vile trick.'

'An old war ruse, Marquis. The lion is in the trap.'

'Why, you despicable old monk, I'm tempted to run you through with my sword.'

He opened his long, skeletal arms, revealing his chest, and said in a trembling voice:

'Please do. My corpse will speak for me.'

'That's enough.'

'Will you give me that money?'

'Yes.'

'When?'

'Tomorrow.'

He said nothing for a moment and then insisted in a tone that was at once timid and insistent:

'It has to be now.'

'Isn't my word good enough?'

Almost humbly, he murmured:

'I don't doubt your word, but it has to be now. I might not have the courage to face you tomorrow. Besides, I want to leave Estella this very night. That money is not for me; I'm no thief. I need it in order to rejoin the troops. I will leave you a signed note. I have longstanding commitments to certain people and I had to do something. Brother Ambrosio never breaks his word.'

I said to him sadly:

'Why couldn't you ask me for the money as a friend?'

He sighed:

'I didn't dare. I don't know how to ask for anything. It makes me feel ashamed. I would find it easier to kill someone than to ask for something. I'm not doing this out of any ill feeling, it's just sheer embarrassment.'

His voice broke; he stopped talking and went out into the street, oblivious to the drenching rain. Trembling with fear, the maid led me to where her lady was waiting.

María Antonieta had just arrived and was sitting beside a brazier, her hands folded, her hair damp and dishevelled from the rain and mist. When I went in, she looked at me with sad, sombre eyes, ringed with dark shadows.

'Why did you insist on coming tonight?'

Wounded by the indifference of her words, I stood still in the middle of the room.

'I regret to say that it was all a story dreamed up by your chaplain.'

She insisted:

'When I came home, I found him waiting for me on your orders.'

I said nothing more, resigned to her reproaches, since it would have been ungallant to tell her what had really happened and to explain Brother Ambrosio's ploy to get me there. Her eyes were dry, but her voice was hoarse with emotion.

'Why are you so eager to see me now, when you never once wrote to me while you were away. Have you nothing to say? What do you want?'

Wishing to make amends to her, I said:

'I want you, María Antonieta.'

Her lovely, mystical eyes flashed scornfully.

'You want to compromise me, to take me away from the Queen's side. You are my executioner.'

I smiled.

'I am your victim.'

I seized her hands and tried to kiss them, but she pulled away fiercely. María Antonieta suffered from what the ancients called 'the sacred illness' and since she had the soul of a saint and the blood of a courtesan, sometimes, in winter, she would renounce love. The poor woman belonged to that race of admirable women who, when they grow old, become edifying figures leading devout lives, yet surrounded by a vague legend of ancient sins. Sombre and sighing, she remained silent, stubbornly staring into space. I again took her hands and held them in mine, though without trying to kiss them, fearful that she might pull away again. In a loving voice, I pleaded:

'María Antonieta!'

She said nothing. After a moment, I said again:

'María Antonieta!'

She turned and, withdrawing her hands, replied coldly:

'What do you want?'

'I want you to tell me all your sorrows.'

'Why?'

'So that I can console you.'

She dropped her mask of inscrutability and, suddenly fierce and passionate, she leaned towards me and cried out:

'Just count up all your ungrateful acts, because those are my sorrows.'

The flame of love burned in her eyes with a solemn fire that seemed to consume her. Hers were the mystical eyes that you occasionally glimpse in convent parlours. She said in a low voice:

'My husband is coming to serve as an aide to the King.'

'Where has he been?'

'With the Infante Don Alfonso.'

I murmured:

'That *is* a nuisance.'

'It's more than a nuisance. It means that we'll have to live together. The Queen is forcing it on me; I would rather return to Italy than live with him. Have you nothing to say?'

'I can only submit to your will.'

She gave me an intense look.

'Would you be capable of sharing me between the two of you? Good God, I wish I were a withered, old woman.'

I gratefully kissed the hands of my adored love. I have never felt jealous of any husband, but those scruples on her part had a special charm, perhaps the best that María Antonieta could offer me. One does not reach old age without having learned that tears, regrets and blood exude an aphrodisiac essence that

122

prolongs the pleasure of love affairs – a sacred numen that heightens lust, the mother of divine silence and the mother of the world. How often, during that night, did I taste María Antonieta's tears on my lips. I still recall the sweet, lamenting voice with which she whispered in my ear, her eyelids trembling, her mouth quivering, her breath and her words filling mine:

'I shouldn't love you. I should smother you in my arms, like this, like this . . .'

I sighed:

'Your arms are like a divine halter about my neck.'

And, holding me still closer, she moaned:

'Oh, how I love you! Why do I love you so much? What love potion have you given me? You are my madness! Say something, say something!'

'I prefer to listen to you.'

'But I want you to say something!'

'I would only say what you already know, that I am dying of love for you.'

María Antonieta kissed me again, then, smiling and blushing, said quietly:

'The night is very long.'

'My absence was much longer.'

'I bet you've deceived me endlessly!'

'I'll show you that's not true.'

Still red-faced and laughing, she replied:

'You'd better watch what you say.'

'You'll see.'

'I can be very demanding.'

I confess that when I heard that, I trembled, for my nights were no longer as triumphant as they had been on those tropical nights perfumed by La Niña Chole's passion. María Antonieta freed herself from my arms and went into her boudoir. I waited a while and then followed her. She heard my footsteps and I saw her white figure run away and hide behind the drapes about her bed, an ancient bed of polished walnut, the classic nuptial bed in which noble couples in Navarre would sleep until they reached old age, chaste, simple,

Christian, ignorant of the voluptuous art that tickled the malign and somewhat theological wit of my teacher Aretino. María Antonieta was as demanding as a doge's wife, but I was as wise as an old cardinal who has learned the secret arts of love in the confessional and in some Renaissance court. Sighing and swooning, she said:

'Xavier, this is the last time!'

I thought she was referring to our amorous deeds and, since I still felt capable of renewed efforts, I sighed and, with the lightest of kisses, aroused the strawberry nipple of one breast. She sighed too and folded her bare arms, resting her hands on her shoulders like one of those penitent saints depicted in ancient paintings.

'Xavier, when will we see each other again?'

'Tomorrow.'

'No, tomorrow my calvary begins.'

She fell silent for a moment and, placing the loving knot of her arms about my neck, she murmured:

'The Queen is determined that there should be a reconciliation, but I swear to you that never . . . I'll defend myself by saying that I'm ill.'

Yes, the illness that María Antonieta suffered from was indeed a sacred one. That night she moaned in my arms like the ancient goddess Fauna. The divine María Antonieta was very passionate, and passionate women are always easily deceived. God, who knows everything, knows that such women are not to be feared; rather one should fear those languid, sighing women, more anxious to give pleasure to their lover than to take pleasure themselves. María Antonieta was as frank and selfish as a child, and in her moments of transporting passion she entirely forgot about me. At such moments – her breasts trembling like two white doves, her eyes clouded, her half-open mouth revealing the cool whiteness of her teeth between the fiery roses of her lips – hers was an incomparably sensual, fecund beauty, of a sort steeped in eighteenth-century literature.

When I left María Antonieta, day was not yet breaking though the bugles were already sounding reveille. The moon still cast its sad, sepulchral light on the snowy city. Not knowing where to find lodging at that hour, I wandered the streets and happened upon the square where Brother Ambrosio lived. I stopped beneath the wooden balcony to shelter from the drizzling rain that was once again beginning to fall, and after a while, I noticed that the door was ajar, buffeted by the wild, bitter wind. It was such a foul night that, without even thinking about it, I decided to go in, feeling my way to the stairs, while the greyhound in the stables barked furiously, rattling its chain. Brother Ambrosio appeared at the top of the stairs, carrying a large candle. His long, scrawny body was adorned with a tattered cassock and, on his trembling head, he wore a black, pointed cap, which made him look like some kind of grotesque astrologer. With sombre resolve, without saying a word, I went in and he followed, holding the candle aloft to light the corridor. Inside, I could hear the dull murmur of voices and of money changing hands. A few men were gathered in the room playing cards; they had their hats on and their cloaks slung loosely across their shoulders. From their clean-shaven faces it was clear that they were members of the clergy. The pack was in the hands of a sallow, snub-nosed knave who was just putting two cards down on the table as I entered the room:

'Lay your bets.'

A devout voice murmured:

'Aha, a Queen!'

And another voice whispered as if in the confessional:

'What are we looking for?'

'Can't you see? A court card! He's dealt seven of them already.'

The man holding the pack said sternly:

'Please don't discuss the value of the cards. That's no way to go on. Everyone then bets on the same one!'

A toothless old man wearing spectacles said in a calm, evangelical voice:

'Don't get so upset, Miquelcho, to each his own. Don Nicolás thinks it's court cards . . .'

Don Nicolás said:

'He's dealt seven of them already.'

'Nine actually . . . but they're not court cards, they're number cards, that's what we're playing.'

There was a murmur of other voices, like a litany:

'It's your turn, Miquelcho.'

'Take no notice.'

'We'll see what we'll see.'

'Aren't you going to deal the next two cards?'

Miquelcho said in surly voice:

'No.'

Then he started to lay down the cards. Everyone fell silent. A few of those present swivelled round irritably, gave me a quick glance, then turned their attention back to the cards. Brother Ambrosio gestured to the seminarian, who was shuffling the cards. He put them down and came over. Brother Ambrosio said:

'Marquis, please, for the love of God, don't remind me about what happened earlier tonight. I'd spent all afternoon drinking just to get up enough nerve to do it.'

He stammered out a few more confused words, then placed a gnarled hand on the shoulder of the seminarian, who had joined us and was listening. Brother Ambrosio said with a sigh:

'It's all his fault. I'm taking him along as my lieutenant when I leave.'

Miquelcho fixed me with bold eyes and felt in his pockets for his tobacco.

'We had to get the money from somewhere. Brother Ambrosio told me how generous his friend and protector was . . .'

Brother Ambrosio opened his black mouth in rough praise:

'Extremely generous! In that respect, as in everything, he's the finest gentleman in all Spain.'

Some of the players were eyeing us curiously. Miquelcho moved away, picked up his cards and continued shuffling them. When he had finished, he said to the old man with the spectacles:

'Cut the cards, Don Quintiliano.'

As he picked up the pack with trembling hand, Don Quintiliano said, smiling:

'Watch out now, it's bound to be an ace.'

Miquelcho put another two cards on the table and turned to me:

'I won't ask you to play because there's absolutely no money in it.'

And the old man in the spectacles added in the same evangelical tone:

'We're all very poor.'

And another murmured sententiously:

'Here you can only win pennies, but you can lose millions.'

Seeing me hesitate, Miquelcho stood up, offering me the pack, and all the clergymen made room for me at the table. I turned, smiling, to Brother Ambrosio.

'Brother Ambrosio, I have a feeling that your money is going to stay right here.'

'God forbid. Right, that's it, the game's over, now.'

And with that, he blew out the candle. The dawn light filtered in through the windows, and the sound of bugles rose up above the hollow sound of horses trotting over the cobbles in the city squares. It was a patrol of Bourbon lancers.

Despite the strong winds and heavy snow, Don Carlos had resolved to go on a campaign. I was told that, for some time now, all they had been waiting for in order to set off was the arrival of the Bourbon cavalry – three hundred veteran lancers, who later richly deserved their name 'the lancers of El Cid'. The Count of Volfani, who had arrived with them, was among the King's aides. We were both very pleased to see each other, for we were great friends, as you can imagine, and we rode along together. The bugles sounded the order to march, the wind ruffled the horses' manes, and the people gathered in the street to cheer us on:

'Long live Carlos VII!'

Every so often, some old woman would lean out from one of the narrow windows high up beneath the blackened eaves and, holding open the latch with one withered hand, would cry out almost angrily:

'Long live the King of all good Christians!'

And the robust voice of the people would reply:

'Viva!'

We paused for a moment on the road. A wild, tempestuous, icy wind blowing down from the mountains beat against us; our capes flapped about us and our berets, pushed back on our heads and revealing tanned foreheads, gave us a look of magnificent, tragic fury. Some of the horses neighed and reared up, and we all steadied ourselves in the saddle. Then the whole column set off along the road that wound away between hills crowned with chapels. We were continually buffeted by great gusts of wind and rain, and so the order was given to stop in the village of Zabalcín. The royal headquarters was a large farmhouse situated where two very rough roads met, one a carriageway and the other a bridle path. Soon after we had dismounted, we all gathered in the kitchen by the fire, and an old woman ran through the house in order to fetch the high-backed chair in which her grandfather used to sit and to offer it to the King. The rain beat hard and incessantly against the windows, and our conversation consisted mainly of complaints about the awful weather that was preventing us from meting out due punishment to the pro-Alfonso faction occupying the road to Oteiza. Luckily, as darkness fell, the storm died away. Don Carlos whispered to me:

'Bradomín, what shall we do so as not to get bored?'

I replied:

'Sir, the women here are all old. Shall we perhaps say the rosary together?'

The King fixed me with mocking, penetrating eyes.

'Why don't you read us that sonnet you composed for my cousin Alfonso. Get up on that chair.'

The courtiers all laughed. I sat for a moment looking at them and then, bowing to the King, said:

'Sir, I make rather a high-born minstrel.'

Don Carlos hesitated at first, then, smiling, came over and embraced me:

'Bradomín, I did not mean to offend you, you know that, don't you?'

'I do, sir, but I was afraid that others might not.'

The King glanced about at his retinue and said in his severe, majestic tones:

'Yes, you're right.'

There was a long silence, broken only by the gusting wind and the crackle of flames in the chimney. The kitchen was filling up with shadows, but through the dripping window panes, you could see that outside it was still only late afternoon. The two roads – the bridle path and the carriageway – disappeared amongst jagged rocks and, at that hour, both seemed equally solitary. With a mysterious gesture, Don Carlos called me over to the window where he was standing.

'Bradomín, you and Volfani will accompany me. We're going to Estella, but it is vital that no one else should know.'

Suppressing a smile, I asked:

'Sir, do you want me to tell Volfani?'

'Volfani already knows, since he was the one who organised the party.'

I bowed, murmuring some words of praise for my friend.

'Sir, I'm delighted to see you do such justice to the Count's great talents.'

The King kept silent, as if wishing to show his displeasure at my words. Then opening the window and reaching out his hand, he said:

'It's stopped raining.'

The moon was just visible in the cloudy sky. Shortly afterwards, Volfani arrived:

'Everything is ready, sir.'

The King said:

'Let's wait until nightfall.'

In the darkness of the kitchen, two voices boomed out: Don Antonio Lizárraga and Don Antonio Dorregaray were discussing the military arts. They were remembering battles won and forging hopes for new triumphs. Dorregaray grew emotional when he spoke about soldiers. He pondered the serene courage of Castilians, the bravery of Catalans and the sheer vigour of men from Navarre. Suddenly an autocratic voice broke in:

'The best soldiers in the world.'

And on the other side of the fire, the bent figure of old General Aguirre rose slowly to his feet. The reddish glow of the flames flickered on his wrinkled face, and his eyes shone with youthful fire beneath the thick snow of his eyebrows. In a trembling voice, as emotional as a child's, he went on:

'Navarre is the true Spain. Only here do you find the same loyalty, faith and heroism as there was in the days of our greatness.'

There were tears in his voice. He too belonged to another age. I confess that I admire these ingenuous souls, who still trust in the old, austere virtues for the good fortune of the people. I admire and pity them, because they are completely blind to the fact that the people, like all mortals, are only happy when they forget about what we call historical consciousness in favour of that blind instinct for the future that is above good and evil and that triumphs even over death. The day will come, though, when there emerges in the conscience

130

of the living a sense of remorse for the harsh sentence that condemns those as yet unborn. We are a land of transcendental sinners who have set a fool's cap on the yellowing skull that once filled the souls of ancient hermits with sombre thoughts. Is this not a land of elegant cynics, breaking all the laws – even the supreme law that unites the ants with the stars – by refusing to create new life and preparing themselves instead for death in some bright seaside resort! Would that not perhaps be the most amusing way to end the world, with the coronation of Sappho and Ganymede? By this time, it was night, and moonlight was falling on the window sill. Through the open window came a cold, damp breeze that made the flames in the fireplace rise up only to shrink back. Don Carlos indicated to us that we should follow him. We went out and walked for a while until we reached the shelter of some rocks where a soldier was waiting with some horses. The King mounted and galloped off, and we galloped after him. As we passed some guards, a voice in the night called out:

'Who goes there?'

And the soldier shouted back:

'Carlos VII!'

'What is the password?'

'The house of Bourbon!'

And they let us through. The rocks flanking the road seemed full of menace and, from the nearby hillside, in the silence of the night, we heard the murmur of swollen streams. At the city gates we had to leave the horses with the soldier and proceed cautiously on foot.

We stopped outside a large old house with barred windows – the house of my lovely dancer now elevated to the status of Duchess of Uclés. We knocked cautiously, and the door opened. The great iron lantern was lit, and a man marched ahead of us, opening other doors that remained open long after we had passed through them. More than once, the man glanced at me curiously. I was looking at him, too, wondering who he was. He had a wooden leg and was tall and gaunt with dark Spanish eyes and the bald head and profile of a Caesar. I felt a sudden flash of recognition when I noticed the occasional solemn gesture with which he smoothed down the one tuft of hair above his forehead. The Caesar with the wooden leg had been a famous pica-dor, a man of immense charm, and a great one for parties with flamenco singers and aristocrats. It was once said that he had replaced me in the lovely dancer's affections. I never attempted to verify the truth of this because I have always felt it was the duty of knights-errant to respect the minor secrets of the female heart. With what deep melancholy did I remember those happy times! They seemed to stir into life again at the thud of that wooden leg on the floor as we walked down the vast corridor on whose walls hung old paintings depicting the love affair between Doña Marina and Hernán Cortés. My heart was still beating fast when the Duchess emerged from a door at the far end of the corridor. Don Carlos asked her:

'Has she come?'

'She won't be long, sir.'

The Duchess made as if to step aside, but the King gallantly refused:

'Please, ladies first.'

The room, only dimly lit by the candelabra on the tables, was large and cold, with a polished wooden floor. A copper brazier, perched on lion's feet, stood in front of the sofa in the reception room. As he stretched out his hands to warm them, Don Carlos muttered:

'The only thing women are good at is keeping people waiting. That is their one great talent.'

He fell silent and we respected that silence. The Duchess smiled at me. Seeing her in her widow's weeds, I remembered the woman in the black veil whom I had seen leaving the church in Doña Margarita's retinue. The thud of the wooden leg came echoing down the corridor again, accompanied by a murmur of voices. Shortly afterwards, two women came in, breathing hard and swathed in cloaks still damp from the night air. When they saw us, one of them stepped back, clearly annoyed. Don Carlos went over and, after saying a few words to her in a low voice, they left the room together. The other, a duenna, followed noiselessly only to return shortly afterwards. With one hand, barely visible beneath her cloak, she signalled to Volfani who got up and went out after her. Finding ourselves alone, the duchess laughed and said in a low voice:

'They won't show their faces because you're here.'

'Do I know them then?'

'I don't know . . . Don't ask.'

Feeling not the slightest curiosity, I said nothing and tried instead to kiss my friend's aristocratic hands, but she drew back, smiling.

'Behave yourself. We're too old for such things.'

'You, Carmen, are eternally young!'

She looked at me for a moment and gave a cruel, mischievous reply:

'Well, I can't say the same for you.'

Then, taking pity on me and wanting to staunch the wound she had inflicted, she threw her sable boa around my neck and offered me her lips like a fruit – divine lips that dissolved into perfumed prayers and flamenco cries of *Olé*! She pulled away suddenly because she heard the thud of the wooden leg returning, echoing through the great, rambling house. I said, smiling:

'What are you afraid of?'

Her pretty brow pleated into a frown and she said:

'Nothing. Don't tell me you believe the rumour too?'

And crossing herself, she murmured with a mixture of piety and coquetry:

'I swear to you, there's never been anything between him and me. We're from the same part of Andalusia and I feel a great loyalty towards him; that's why, when he was gored by a bull and couldn't work anymore, I took him in out of charity. You would do the same.'

'Of course,' I said solemnly, although I wasn't entirely sure that I would.

As if wishing to expunge the memory completely, she said by way of an affectionate reproach:

'You haven't even asked me about our daughter.'

For a moment, I was stunned, because I had more or less forgotten. Then my heart placed this excuse on my lips.

'I didn't dare to.'

'Why?'

'I didn't like to mention her while I was here on one of the King's romantic adventures.'

Sadness clouded her eyes.

'She's not here with me. She's in a convent.'

I suddenly sensed the love of that distant, almost illusory daughter.

'Does she look like you?'

'No . . . she's dreadfully plain.'

Fearing that this might all be a joke, I laughed:

'Is she really my daughter?'

The Duchess of Uclés again swore that she was, crossing herself and kissing the tips of her fingers; perhaps I was blinded by my own emotions, but there seemed to me to be no deceit in that oath. Fixing me with her great, dark eyes, she said with all the feeling and charm that you encounter in certain gypsy songs:

'The child is as much my daughter as she is yours. I've never hidden the fact, not even from my husband. He adored her!'

She wiped away a tear. She had been a widow since the beginning of the war, during which the peace-loving Duke had died in obscure circumstances. The former dancer, as faithful to tradition as any grand lady, was bankrupting herself for the cause. She alone had paid for weapons and saddles for a hundred horsemen, a hundred lancers who were called Don Jaime's lancers. When she mentioned the heir to the throne, she softened visibly as if he too were her child:

'So you've seen my precious prince?'

'I have.'

'And which of the Infantas did you meet?'

'Doña Blanca.'

'She's a funny little thing, isn't she? She's going to be a real charmer.'

And that gracious prophecy was still fluttering in the air when we heard the voice of the King at the far end of the room. The duchess stood up.

'What's wrong?'

Don Carlos came in looking rather pale and, seeing our questioning eyes, he explained:

'Something's happened to Volfani. The two ladies had just left and I was talking to him, when I noticed that he was gradually crumpling up in his seat, until he was bent double over the arm of his chair. I had to hold him up.'

Having said that, he left the room, and, in obedience to his unspoken order, we followed. Volfani was sitting in an arm-chair, looking exhausted, shrunken, bent, his head lolling. Don Carlos went over to him and used his strong arms to lift him into a more comfortable position.

'How are you, Volfani?'

Volfani made a visible effort to reply, but was unable to. Strings of saliva hung from his inert, gaping mouth. The duchess hurriedly wiped the saliva away, as sublime and charitable as a St Veronica. Volfani looked at us with sad, mortal eyes. With the courage that women often show in such circumstances, the Duchess said:

'Don't worry, Count, it's nothing serious. The same thing happened to my husband once, he was a bit overweight and . . .'

Volfani waved one limp arm and from his lips there came a

groan which was clearly an attempt to speak. We looked at each other, convinced that he was dying. The same groan, accompanied by a few bubbles of spit, issued from Volfani's lips. From his clouded eyes two brief tears ran down his waxen face. Don Carlos spoke to him as to a child, in a voice loud with affectionate authority:

'We'll take you back to your own house. Do you want Bradomín to go with you?'

Volfani said nothing. The King took us to one side and we spoke together in low voices. First, as befitted magnanimous, Christian hearts, we all said how dreadful for poor María Antonieta. Next, we all predicted the imminent death of poor Volfani. Lastly, we pondered how best to get him to his house without arousing comment. The Duchess said that, of course, none of her servants could take him, and she was doubtless right; then, after some discussion, it was agreed to entrust him to Rafael el Rondeño. When he learned of this, the Caesar of the wooden leg smoothed his tuft of hair and said:

'Are you sure he's not just had too much wine?'

The Duchess, with justifiable indignation, told him to be quiet. The Caesar, utterly impassive, continued stroking his hair, then turned to us and offered a solution to the problem. The two sergeants who were currently lodging in the attic could take the Count. They were trustworthy men, veterans from the Fifth Navarre regiment, and they would accompany him to his house as if they were merely on their way home together. He rounded off his speech with the word *¿Hace?* – 'All right?' – as redolent of his former swaggering, bullfighting life as a tall glass of manzanilla.

We went back to where we had left the horses. The King could not conceal his distress. He kept repeating the same sad phrase:

'Poor Volfani, he had such a loyal heart.'

For a while, all you could hear was the sound of horses' hooves. The moon, a bright winter moon, lit the snowy, arid slopes of Monte-Jurra. The cold, squally wind beat in our faces. Don Carlos said something and a gust of wind scattered his words. All I heard was:

'Do you think he'll die?'

Cupping one hand over my mouth, I shouted:

'I'm afraid so, sir!'

And an echo repeated those words, blurred and shapeless. Don Carlos fell silent and did not speak for the rest of the journey. We dismounted in the shelter of the rocks near the farmhouse and, handing over the reins to the soldier who had accompanied us, we continued on foot. At the door, we stopped for a moment to study the black clouds that the wind was blowing across the face of the moon. Don Carlos said:

'Wretched weather! He had such a loyal heart.'

Before going in, he gave one last look at the stormy sky heavy with the promise of more snow. Once across the threshold, we heard the sound of voices arguing. I said to the King, to calm him:

'It's nothing, sir. They're just gambling away their future wages.'

Don Carlos gave an indulgent laugh.

'Do you know who they are?'

'I can guess, sir. The entire barracks.'

We had gone into the room set aside for the King. A large candle was on the table, the bed was covered by a moleskin blanket, and the brazier, set between two camp chairs, was burning low. Sitting down to rest, Don Carlos said with affectionate irony:

'You know, Bradomín, tonight someone warned me about you. They said that your friendship brings misfortune. They begged me to distance myself from you.'

I murmured, smiling:

'Was it a lady, sir?'

'A lady who doesn't actually know you, but who says that her grandmother always cursed you as the worst of all men.'

I felt a vague feeling of apprehension.

'Who was her grandmother, sir?'

'A princess from Romagna.'

I said nothing, overcome with emotion. The saddest memory of my whole life had just risen up in my soul, piercing it through with mortal cold. I left the room with my soul in mourning. That hatred transmitted to her granddaughter by an old lady, reminded me of the first and greatest love of my life lost for ever in my ill-starred fortunes. With what sadness I remembered my youthful years in Italy, when I served in the Pope's guard. I had arrived at the old papal city on a spring morning filled with the trembling voices of bells and smelling of newly opened roses, at the palace of a noble princess, who received me surrounded by her daughters, as if in a Court of Love. That memory filled my soul. The whole tumultuous, sterile past engulfed me, drowning me in its bitter waters.

Wanting to be alone, I went out into the garden, and for a long time I walked my solitude and my sadness up and down in the quiet night, beneath the moon, which had been a witness on other occasions to my loves and glories. Hearing the sound of the swollen torrents rushing down to flood the roads, I compared them to my life, sometimes roaring with passions, at others a dried-up, arid river bed. Since the moon did nothing to dissipate my black thoughts, I realised that I would have to seek oblivion elsewhere, and with a resigned sigh, I joined my worldly friends in the barracks. It is a sad fact, but the white moon offers fewer consolations to the sorrowing heart than a game of cards. At cockcrow, the bugles sounded reveille, and I had to put away my winnings and immerse myself once more in sentimental thoughts. Shortly afterwards, an aide came to tell me that the King wanted to see me. I found him in his room, sipping a cup of coffee, his spurs and sabre already buckled on:

'I'll be with you in a moment, Bradomín.'

'At your orders, sir.'

The King drank the last drop of coffee and then, putting down his cup, he led me over to the window.

'It seems we have yet another troublesome priest on our hands. A loyal, valiant man, they say, but a fanatic. The priest from Orio.'

I said:

'Is he emulating Santa Cruz?'

'No, he's just a poor old man for whom the years have not passed, and who wages war as they did in the time of my grandfather. It seems he intends having two mad Russian travellers burned as heretics. I want you to see him, and make him realise that times have changed. Tell him to go back to his church and give up his prisoners. As you know, I have no desire to upset Russia.'

'And what if he proves stubborn?'

Don Carlos smiled majestically:

'I leave that up to you.'

And he moved off to receive a courier who had just arrived. I stayed where I was, awaiting one final word. Don Carlos looked up for a moment from the report he was reading and gave me one of his looks — friendly, noble, serene, sad — the look of a great King.

I left his room and, a moment later, I was riding along with an escort of ten lancers chosen from the Bourbon ranks. We did not stop until we reached San Pelayo de Ariza. There I learned that a pro-Alfonso faction had cut off the bridge at Omellín. I asked if it was possible to cross the river and they told me no. After the recent heavy rains the ford was impassable and the ferry boat had been set fire to. That meant going back and following the mountain road round to cross the river at the bridge of Arnáiz. I wanted, above all, to complete the mission with which I had been entrusted, and I did not hesitate, even though the route was full of dangers, something which the guide was careful to point out to me; he was an old villager with three young sons in Don Carlos' army.

Before setting out, we took our horses down to the river to drink and, seeing the other shore so close, I felt tempted to risk a crossing. I consulted the men, and since some seemed determined to follow me whilst others hesitated, I put an end to all the talk and rode into the river myself. My horse trembled and its ears quivered. The water was already up to its girth when, on the other shore, I saw an old woman laden with firewood who began shouting to us. At first, I thought that she was warning us about the danger of trying to ford the river, then, when I was halfway across, I heard what she was saying.

'Stay where you are, gentlemen. For God's sake, don't cross. The road ahead is crawling with *alfonsistas*.'

And throwing down her bundle of wood, she waded into the water in her clogs, her arms upstretched like a village sibyl – clamorous, desperate, tragic.

'Our Lord God wants to test us, to find out how much faith we each have in our souls, to prove our resolve. All they talk about is the great battle they've won. Abuín, Tafal, Endrás, Otáiz have all fallen to the enemy.'

I turned round to judge the mood of my men only to find

that they were all beating a cowardly retreat. At that same moment, I heard shots and saw the circles left by bullets in the water around me. I hurriedly turned back, and just as my horse's hooves reached the shore, I felt a bullet pierce my left arm and the warm blood pour down over my numb hand. Bent over their saddles, my horsemen were galloping up a hill through thick, damp vegetation. We entered the village, our horses covered in sweat. I called for the local quack who set my arm using four bamboo canes and then, taking no rest or any other precautions, I led my ten lancers into the hills. The guide, who was walking ahead of my horse, kept warning me of new dangers.

The pain from my wounded arm was so great that the soldiers in my escort kept a respectful silence, seeing my feverish eyes, my waxen face, my dark beard, which seemed to have grown in a matter of hours the way that the beards on corpses grow. The pain was so intense that I could barely see, and I rode with the reins loose over the saddle, so that as we rode through a village, I nearly knocked down two women who were walking along together, almost hurling them into the mud. As they drew away, they shouted out, fixing me with frightened eyes. One of the women recognised me.

'Marquis!'

I turned with a look of pained indifference:

'What do you want, Señora?'

'Don't you remember me?'

She came over, uncovering her head a little, for she was wearing the traditional headscarf of a Navarre village woman. I saw a lined face and a pair of dark eyes, those of someone good-hearted and energetic. I struggled to remember:

'Is it you?'

I hesitated. She came to my aid.

'It's Sister Simona, Marquis! Surely you remember?'

My memory gone, I repeated:

'Sister Simona.'

You saw me a hundred times when we were on the frontier with the King! But what's wrong? Are you wounded?'

I merely showed her my livid hand, my fingernails now

cold and tinged with blue. She examined it a moment and then declared in kindly, vigorous terms:

'You can't ride on in that condition, Marquis.'

I murmured:

'I have orders from the King.'

'I don't care how many orders you've got. I've seen a lot of wounds in this war, and I can tell you that that arm won't wait. So let the King wait.'

And she took the reins of my horse and led him away. In that lined, brown face, her dark, blazing eyes, the eyes of a born founder of convents, were full of tears. Turning to my soldiers, she said:

'Follow me, lads.'

She spoke in that tender, authoritative tone that I had so often heard in the voices of grandmothers, the eldest daughters of their families. Even though the pain had drained me of all my energy, out of gallant habit I tried to dismount. Sister Simona would have none of it, and she said so in brusque but affectionate terms. Lacking all will, I obeyed and we rode down a street lined with gardens and low hovels, their chimneys smoking in the peace of the afternoon and filling the air with the smell of burnt pine needles. As if in a dream, I heard the voices of children playing and the angry shouts of mothers. The branches of a willow tree, overhanging a wall, struck me in the face. Bending low in my saddle, I passed beneath its baleful shade.

We stopped outside a grand house with a coat of arms carved in stone above the door and with an ample, musty-smelling hallway, which seemed to proclaim a generous spirit. It stood in an empty, grass-grown square that echoed to the sounds of a blacksmith's hammer and an old woman singing as she darned her underskirt. As Sister Simona helped me dismount, she said:

'This has been our home ever since the republicans burned down the convent at Abarzuza out of rage at the death of their general . . . !'

I asked vaguely:

'Which general?'

'Don Manuel de la Concha!'

Then I remembered having heard, where or when I did not know, how the news had been carried to Estella by a nun disguised as a village woman. To gain time, the nun had walked all night in the middle of a storm and, when she arrived, people had taken her for a visionary. That nun was Sister Simona. When I reminded her of it, she said, smiling:

'Ah, Marquis, I thought they would shoot me that night.'

Leaning on her shoulder, I went up the broad stone staircase and ahead of us went Sister Simona's companion, who was little more than a child, with velvet eyes, very sweet and loving. She knocked at the door and the sister who was acting as porter opened it:

'Deo gratias!'

'Deo gratias!'

Sister Simona said to me:

'This is our field hospital.'

In the twilight depths of a white room with a wooden floor, a group of women in wimples, sitting on low wicker chairs, were making cotton wool out of threads and tearing up bandages. Sister Simona said:

143

'Make up a bed in the cell that belonged to Don Antonio Dorregaray.'

Two nuns got up and went out. One of them had a great bunch of keys at her waist. Sister Simona, helped by the girl who had accompanied her, began undoing the bandage on my arm.

'Let's see what it looks like. Who put these splints on you?'

'A local man in San Pelayo de Ariza.'

'Good God! Is it very painful?'

'It is.'

Once the splints were off, I felt a sense of relief, and I sat up with a burst of sudden energy.

'Just patch me up and I'll be on my way.'

Sister Simona said calmly:

'Sit down and don't be so stupid. Tell me what this order from the King is and, if necessary, I'll see to it myself.'

I sat down, giving in to the nun's calm tones.

'What town is this?'

'Villarreal de Navarra.'

'How far is it from Amelzu?'

'Six leagues.'

Suppressing a groan, I said:

'The orders I have are for the priest in Orio.'

'And what are they?'

'For him to deliver some prisoners over to me. I have to see him today.'

Sister Simona shook her head.

'I've told you before not to be so stupid. I'll sort it out. Who are these prisoners?'

'Two foreigners he wants to have burned as heretics.'

The nun laughed uproariously.

'He gets some strange ideas that priest!'

Suppressing another moan, I laughed too. For a moment, my eyes met the eyes of the young girl, who, frightened and compassionate, had just looked up from my yellowish arm and the purple hole left by the bullet. Sister Simona said to her in a low voice:

'Maximina, make sure you put linen sheets on the Marquis' bed.'

She hurried out of the room and Sister Simona said to me:

'I could see she was on the verge of tears. She's an angel that girl.'

I felt my soul fill with tenderness for the girl with the sad, compassionate, velvet eyes. My febrile memory began stubbornly, insistently to repeat:

'She's dreadfully plain, plain, plain!'

With the help of a soldier and an old serving woman who worked for the nuns, I got into bed. Sister Simona arrived soon afterwards and, sitting down at the head of the bed, she began:

'I've sent word to the mayor telling him to find lodgings for the men who were with you. The doctor will be here in a moment; he's just finishing his rounds in another ward.'

I nodded and gave a faint smile. Shortly afterwards, we heard a hoarse, familiar voice in the corridor talking to the nuns, who responded in mellifluous tones. Sister Simona muttered:

'Here he is.'

Some time passed, though, before the doctor looked round the door, humming a popular Basque tune. He was a jovial old man, with bright red cheeks and expressive eyes, full of innocent mischief. Pausing on the threshold, he exclaimed:

'What should I do? Should I remove my beret?'

I murmured weakly:

'No, sir.'

'Well, I won't then, although the person who should say yea or nay around here is the Mother Superior. Now let's see what's wrong with the valiant corporal.'

Sister Simona said with all the primness of an old lady:

'This "corporal" is the Marquis of Bradomín.'

The old man's bright eyes looked at me attentively.

'I've heard a lot about you.'

He fell silent, bending over to examine my hand, and as he started to undo the bandage, he turned for a moment.

'Sister Simona, would you mind bringing the light a little closer?'

The nun did so. The doctor bared my arm to the shoulder

and ran his hands over it, squeezing it. Surprised, he looked up:

'Doesn't it hurt?'

I said dully:

'A bit.'

'Well, shout out then. That's the purpose of the examination – to find out where it hurts.'

He began again, stopping now and then and looking into my face. He pressed harder with his fingers around the edge of the actual bullet wound.

'Does it hurt here?'

'Yes, a lot.'

He pressed harder and there was a crunch of bones. A shadow seemed to pass over the doctor's face and, addressing Sister Simona, who was standing motionless holding the light, he said:

'He has a comminuted fracture of the ulna and the radius.'

Sister Simona nodded. The doctor carefully rolled down my sleeve and, looking me in the eye, said.

'I can see that you're a brave man.'

I smiled wanly and there was a moment of silence. Sister Simona put the lamp down on the table and returned to my bedside. I saw them in the shadows, intent and serious. Understanding the reason for that silence, I said:

'Will you have to amputate?'

The doctor and the nun looked at each other. I read the sentence in their eyes and my only thought was what attitude I should adopt from then on, when in the company of women, in order to make the loss of my arm seem poetic. If only I could have lost it during one of our history's more exalted moments! I confess that I felt more envious then of Cervantes' glorious career as a soldier, than I did of his achievement in having written *Don Quixote*. While I was thinking these mad thoughts, the doctor again uncovered my arm and explained that the gangrene was so advanced they could not risk any further delay. Sister Simona beckoned him over and I saw them talking together at one end of the room. Then the nun returned to my bedside.

146

'You're going to have to be very brave, Marquis.'

I murmured:

'I will, Sister Simona.'

And the good Mother Superior said again:

'Very brave.'

I looked at her hard and said:

'Poor Sister Simona, you don't know how to tell me.'

The nun said nothing and any vague hopes I had been nurturing fled like a bird into the twilight. My soul felt like an old abandoned nest. The nun whispered:

'One must accept the misfortunes that God sends us.'

She walked softly away and the doctor came over. Slightly warily I said:

'Have you cut off many arms, doctor?'

He smiled and nodded:

'A few, a few.'

Two nuns came in and he went over to help them arrange gauzes and bandages on a table. I followed the preparations with my eyes and, overriding the feminine feeling of self-pity rising up in me, I felt a cruel, bitter pleasure. I was sustained by my one great virtue, pride. I did not complain once, not even when they cut into my flesh, not even when they sawed through the bone, not even when they sewed up the stump. When the last bandage was on, Sister Simona murmured, a glint of sympathetic fire in her eyes:

'I've never seen such bravery.'

And the assistants who had been present at the sacrifice all burst out:

'Such bravery!'

'Such fortitude!'

'And we thought the General was brave!'

I assumed they were congratulating me and said in a feeble voice:

'Thank you, my children.'

And the doctor, who was washing the blood from his hands, told them jovially:

'Leave him to rest now.'

I closed my eyes to hide the two tears welling up in them

and, still without opening them, I noticed that the room had grown dark. I heard a few light steps approaching and then nothing. I don't know if my thoughts merely dissolved into sleep or if I fainted.

All around me was silence and a shadow was watching at my bedside. I opened my eyes in the vague darkness and the shadow approached solicitously. Two sad, compassionate, velvet eyes asked:

'Are you in much pain, sir?'

They were the eyes of the girl, and when I recognised them, I felt as if consoling waters were cooling the scorched desert of my soul. My thoughts flew like a skylark, breaking through the clouds of drowsiness in which there persisted an anxious, painful, confused awareness of reality. I wearily raised my one remaining arm and stroked that head that seemed to be haloed by a divine, childlike sadness. She bent to kiss my hand and when she got up again her velvet eyes were bright with tears. I said to her:

'Don't feel sorry for me, my child.'

She struggled to collect herself and said in a voice charged with emotion:

'You're very brave.'

I smiled, feeling rather flattered by her ingenuous admiration.

'That arm wasn't any use to me anyway.'

The girl looked at me, her lips trembling, her two great eyes fixed on me like two Franciscan flowers giving off a warm, humble perfume. Wanting to savour again the consolation of her shy words, I said:

'You may not realise this, but the fact that we have two arms is like a reminder of less civilised times, when we needed them both in order to climb trees, wrestle with wild animals . . . but nowadays, my dear, you can get by perfectly well with just one. Besides, I hope that this severed branch will help prolong my life, because I am already a very ancient tree.'

The girl sobbed:

'Don't talk like that, please! It makes me so sad.'

Her slightly childish voice had the same soothing charm as

her eyes, whilst her small, pale face with its dark-shadowed eyes hovered hesitantly in the gloom. With my head buried in the pillows, I said weakly:

'Talk to me, my child.'

She replied innocently, almost laughing, as if a gust of childlike joy blew through her words:

'Why do you want me to talk to you?'

'Because it does me good to hear you. Your voice is like a balm to me.'

The girl remained thoughtful for a moment and then, as if she were looking for some hidden meaning in my words, she said:

'Like a balm?'

And sitting in her wicker chair, at the head of my bed, she remained silent, slowly passing the beads of a rosary through her fingers. I could see her through my drooping eyelids as I lay buried in the pit of the hot, burning pillows that seemed to infect me with fever. Little by little, the mists of sleep closed about me again, a weightless, floating sleep, full of crevices and a strange diabolical geometry. I suddenly opened my eyes and the girl said to me:

'The Mother Superior has just left. She told me off because she says I wear you out with my chatter, so you're going to have to keep very quiet.'

She smiled as she spoke and in her sad, wan face, her smile was like the glint of sunlight on humble, dewy flowers. Sitting in her wicker chair, she looked at me with eyes full of melancholy dreams. I felt my soul pierced by a sweet tenderness, innocent as the love of a grandfather who wants only to warm his old age a little by consoling the sorrows of a child and listening to her stories. Merely in order to hear her voice again, I asked:

'What's your name?'

'Maximina.'

'That's a very pretty name.'

She looked at me, blushing furiously, then smiled and said earnestly:

'It's the only pretty thing about me.'

'Your eyes are very pretty too.'

'My eyes maybe, but I'm fairly ordinary otherwise.'

'Oh, I think you're quite something.'

She hurriedly interrupted me:

'No, sir, I'm not. I'm not even very good.'

I held my one hand out to her:

'You're the best girl I've ever met.'

'Girl! I'm practically a dwarf, Marquis. How old do you think I am?'

And standing up, she folded her arms, mocking her own smallness. I said with gentle humour:

'About twenty?'

She looked at me merrily.

'Don't make fun of me. I'm not even fifteen. I thought you were going to say twelve! Oh, but I'm making you talk and the Mother Superior told me not to.'

She sat down hurriedly, raising one finger to her lips, begging forgiveness with her eyes. I again provoked her into talking.

'Have you been a novice long?'

Smiling, she again placed a finger to her lips. Then she said:

'I'm not a novice, I'm a pupil here.'

And sitting there in her chair, she became lost in thought. I fell silent, feeling the charm of those eyes peopled by dreams – the eyes of a girl, the dreams of a woman. The lights of a lost soul in the night-time of my old age!

The loyal troops were marching down the street. You could hear the fanatical roar of the people who had turned out to see them. Some shouted:

'Long live God!'

Others threw their berets in the air and yelled:

'Long live the King! Long live Carlos VII!'

I suddenly remembered the orders I had been given and I tried to sit up, but the pain in my amputated arm brought me up short. It was a dull pain as if my arm were still there, weighing on me like lead. I looked at the girl and said in a sad, mocking voice:

'Sister Maximina, I need the Mother Superior, could you call her for me?'

'She's not here. Can I help you?'

I looked at her, smiling:

'Would you dare to put yourself in great danger for my sake?'

Maximina lowered her eyes and two roses bloomed in her pale cheeks.

'Of course I would.'

'You, my poor little one!'

I said no more, because there was a lump in my throat, from feelings that were at once melancholy and sweet. I sensed that those sad, velvet eyes would be the last to look on me with love. I felt like a dying man contemplating the fiery golds of the evening, knowing that it will be his last. Maximina looked at me and murmured:

'Don't discount me just because I'm small, Marquis.'

I smiled and said:

'You seem very tall to me, my child. I imagine that your eyes gaze on Heaven itself.'

She looked at me, smiling, and then, with a charming seriousness beyond her years, she said:

'You do say some strange things, sir.'

I looked in silence at that head so full of sad, childish charm. After a moment, she asked, with the adorable shyness that made the roses bloom in her cheeks:

'Why did you ask me if I would dare to put myself in danger?'

I smiled.

'That wasn't what I asked you. I asked if you would do so for my sake.'

Maximina said nothing, and I saw her lips tremble and the colour drain from them. After a moment, not daring to look at me, and sitting very still in her chair, her hands folded, she said:

'Are you not my fellow man?'

I sighed.

'Be quiet, my dear, please.'

And I covered my eyes with one hand, in a tragic pose. I remained thus for some time waiting for the girl to question me, but since she said nothing, I decided to be the first to break the long silence:

'Your words have wounded me deeply. They were as cruel as duty itself.'

Maximina murmured:

'Duty is a sweet thing.'

'The duty that comes from the heart is sweet, but not one born of doctrine.'

The sad, velvet eyes looked at me seriously.

'I don't know what you mean, sir.'

And after a moment, she got up to rearrange my pillows, then, saddened to see my stern face, she said:

'What danger were you talking about, Marquis?'

I looked at her, my face still severe.

'It was just a manner of speaking, Sister Maximina.'

'And why did you want to see the Mother Superior?'

'To remind her of an offer she made to me and which she has forgotten.'

Maximina smiled.

'I know what it is. She was to go and see the priest in Orio. But who told you she had forgotten? She came in here to say

153

goodbye to you, and since you were asleep, she didn't want to wake you.'

Maximina ran over to the window. Again the street echoed with the shouts of the people greeting the loyal troops:

'Long live God! Long live the King!'

Maximina sat down on one of the seats by the window, a narrow window with small, greenish panes, the only one in the room. I said to her:

'Why are you sitting so far away, my child?'

'I can hear you just as well from here.'

And from her seat by the window that looked out onto a road lined by withered poplar trees and with a backdrop of sombre, snow-topped mountains, she sent me a glance of compassionate sadness. As in the religious days of the Middle Ages, the voices of the people rose up from the street: Long live God! Long live the King!

Fever troubled my thoughts. I would sleep for a few moments only to wake with a start, feeling, at some remove, the painful gripping of my amputated arm and hand. The whole day passed in the same state of anxiety and tension. Sister Simona came in as night was falling, greeting me in a grave, absolute voice that seemed to contain the very yeast of ancient Castilian virtues.

'How are you feeling, Marquis?'

'Not too good, Sister Simona.'

She vigorously shook the water from her headscarf.

'I had quite a job convincing that priest in Orio.'

I said weakly:

'You saw him then?'

'I've just come from there. A five-hour journey, followed by an hour of sermonising, until I got fed up and told him exactly what I thought of him. God forgive me, I was tempted to scratch his face and pretend I was the Infanta Carlota! I don't even know what I said to him. The poor man had never had any intention of burning the prisoners, he just wanted to keep them with him to see if he could convert them. Anyway, they're here now.'

I sat up on my pillows.

'Would you have them come in, Sister Simona?'

She went over to the door and called:

'Sister Jimena, ask the gentlemen to come in.'

Then, returning to my bedside, she said:

'They're obviously people of quality. One of them is almost a giant. The other is a mere youth, with the face of a young girl, and was doubtless a student in his own land, for he speaks Latin better than the priest himself.'

Hearing the sound of slow, weary footsteps approaching down the corridor, she fell silent and stood waiting, her eyes on the door, where a nun finally appeared. The nun had a deeply lined face and was wearing a very starched habit and a

155

blue apron; her brow and her hands were as white as the host itself.

'Mother, the gentlemen were so tired and numb with cold that I took them to the kitchen to warm up a few scraps for them. They're making short work of the garlic soup I gave them. It looks as if they haven't had a proper meal for three days or more. Have you noticed how you can tell from their hands that they're people of quality?'

Sister Simona replied with a condescending smile:

'I had noticed, yes.'

'One of them is as solemn as a judge, but the other is so handsome you could dress him up as the archangel Raphael in a silk robe with little feathered wings and put him on a float in an Easter procession.'

The Mother Superior was smiling as she listened to the nun, whose limpid, blue eyes beneath wrinkled lids preserved a childlike candour. Sister Simona said in a jolly voice:

'Sister Jimena, I think a good drop of wine would probably go down better with the garlic soup than feathered wings.'

'You're quite right, Mother! I'll see to it at once.'

Sister Jimena shuffled out, her body bent, and Sister Simona watched her leave with kindly eyes.

'Poor Sister Jimena, she's in her second childhood.'

Then she sat down at my bedside and folded her hands. Night was falling, and, through the rain-drenched windows, one could still see the vague outline of the mountains, the snow silvered by the moonlight. Far off, a bugle sounded. Sister Simona said:

'The soldiers who came with you have been causing may-hem. The town is fed up with them and with some other men who arrived yesterday. They beat the notary Arteta because he refused to open up a barrel and invite them to drink the wine, and they wanted to tar and feather Doña Rosa Pedrayes because her husband, who died twenty years ago, was a friend of Espartero. They've apparently ridden their horses up to the top floor of a house and put barley on the tables for them to eat. Terrible.'

I could still hear the vibrant, luminous sound of the bugle

that seemed to be launching its notes upon the air like the unfurling of warlike flags. I felt the warrior spirit rise up in me, despotic and feudal, the atavistic, noble spirit which, had I been born in other times, would have been my downfall. Proud Duque de Alba! Glorious Duque de Sesa, de Terranova y Santangelo! Magnificent Hernán Cortés! In your day, I would have marched under your colours as a second lieutenant. I felt too the beauty of horror; I was filled with love for the glorious red of spilled blood, for the sacking of villages, for cruel old soldiers and those who rape young women, for those who set fire to cornfields and those who commit outrages in the name of military power. Lifting myself up on my pillows, I said as much to Sister Simona.

'Madam, my soldiers are keeping up the tradition of all Castilian lancers, and that tradition is as beautiful as a ballad and as sacred as a religious ritual. And if the honourable inhabitants of Villarreal de Navarra come to me with their complaints, that is what I will say to them.'

In the darkness, I saw Sister Simona wiping away a tear. Her voice heavy with emotion, she said:

'That is exactly what I said, Marquis. Not in those words, because I cannot speak with such eloquence, but in the clear Castilian of my own land. Soldiers should be soldiers, and war should be war.'

At that point, the other older nun, smiling beneath her white, starched robes, timidly opened the door and came in bearing a candle, asking permission to bring in the prisoners. Despite all the years that had passed, I recognised the giant at once. He was the Russian prince who had once provoked my anger, when, in the land of the sun, he had tried to seduce La Niña Chole. Seeing the two prisoners together, I again regretted that I had never chanced to enjoy the beautiful sin, that gift of the gods and temptation of poets. On this occasion, it would have been my war booty and a magnificent revenge, because the giant's companion was the most admirable of youths. Pondering the sad sterility of my fate, I gave a resigned sigh. The youth spoke to me in Latin and on his lips that divine language evoked a happier era when other young men, his fellows, were anointed and crowned with roses by emperors.

'Sir, my father thanks you.'

It was with just that loud, sonorous word 'father' that his brothers would have addressed the emperors. Moved, I said to him:

'May the gods keep you from all evil, my son.'

The two prisoners bowed. I think the giant recognised me, because I caught in his eyes a shifty, cowardly look. I was in no position to exact revenge, and as I watched them leave, I remembered instead the girl with the sad, velvet eyes, and regretted with a sigh that she lacked the graceful forms of that young man.

All night there was noise and the distant firing of rifles. At dawn, the wounded began to arrive, and we learned that the *alfonsistas* had occupied the shrine of San Cernín. The soldiers were covered in mud and their capes smelled damp. They came straggling back along the roads, discouraged and distrustful, muttering that they had been betrayed.

I had obtained permission to get out of bed and I stood with my forehead resting against the window panes, staring out at the mountains that were wrapped in a grey curtain of rain. I felt very weak, and standing there, with my amputated arm, I confess that I was filled by an immense sadness. My pride rose up, and I suffered to think of the pleasure of certain former women friends of whom I will never speak in my memoirs. I spent the whole day in a state of great depression, sitting on one of the seats near the window. The girl with the sad, velvet eyes kept me company for long periods. Once I said to her:

'Sister Maximina, what balm do you bring me today?'

Smiling shyly, she came and sat on the other bench in the window. I took her hand and started to explain to her:

'Sister Maximina, you are the mistress of three balms: one you give with your words, the other with your smiles, the other with your velvet eyes.'

I talked to her like that, in a dull, rather sad voice, as if I were speaking to a child whom I wanted to distract with a fairy tale.

She replied:

'I don't believe you, but I like to hear you talk. No one can talk the way you do about things.'

And she blushed and fell silent. Then she wiped away the condensation from the windows and, looking out into the garden, remained sunk in thought. The garden was a dreary sight. The humble, spontaneous grass of graveyards grew beneath the trees and the rain dripped from their bleak, black, leafless branches. Those pretty birds they call snow birds hopped around the edge of the well, whilst at the foot of the wall a sheep was bleating and straining at the rope tethering it, and a flock of crows flew across the cloudy backdrop of the sky. I said in a low voice:

'Sister Maximina.'

She turned slowly, like a sick child who has lost all pleasure in games.

'What do you want, sir?'

All the sadness of the landscape outside seemed caught in her velvet eyes. I said:

'Sister Maximina, the wounds in my soul are opening and I have need of one of your balms. Which one of them do you want to give me?'

'Whichever you want.'

'The balm from your eyes.'

And I kissed them paternally. She blinked several times and stood there looking very serious, staring down at her delicate, fragile hands, the hands of a child martyr. I felt a deep tenderness filling my soul with a voluptuousness I had never before experienced. It was as if a perfume distilled from tears had flowed into the river of happier times. I said again:

'Sister Maximina.'

Not looking up, she said in a slow, painful voice:

'Yes, Marquis.'

'I think you're very mean with your treasures. Why don't you look at me? Why don't you speak to me? Why don't you smile, Sister Maximina?'

'I was just thinking that you've been standing up a long time. Are you sure you're all right?'

I took her two hands in mine and drew her to me.

'I'll be all right if you give me the gift of your balms.'

For the first time, I kissed her on the lips. They were icy cold. I forgot the sentimental tone of voice I had used up until then and with all the fire of my youthful years, I said:

'Do you think you could love me?'

She shivered but did not reply. I said again:

'Do you think you could love me – with your child's soul?'

160

'Yes, I do love you, I do.'

And she tore herself from my arms, her face contorted. She fled and I did not see her for the rest of the day. I stayed sitting by the window for a long time. The moon was rising over the mountains in a fantastic sky full of heavy clouds. The garden lay in darkness, the house in holy peace. I felt my eyes well with tears. It was the emotion of love which lends a deep sadness to lives that are slowly burning out. As if it were the greatest possible source of happiness, I imagined those tears being wiped away by the girl with the sad, velvet eyes. The murmur of the rosary being said by all the nuns together reached me like an echo from those humble, happy souls who tended the sick as they did the roses in their garden, and who loved our Lord God. Remote and white as a novice escaped from her cell, the solitary moon travelled across the sky. It was Sister Maximina!

After a night struggling with one's sins and one's insomnia, nothing purifies the soul so much as a good bath of prayer and a dawn mass. Prayer then is like the morning dew that douses the fevers of the inferno. Since I have always been a great sinner, I learned this in early life and was unlikely to forget it then. I got up when I heard the nuns ringing the bell, and, kneeling in the chancel, shivering beneath my soldier's tabard, I attended the mass being celebrated by the chaplain. A few tall, gawky lads could be seen kneeling in the shadows along the walls, wrapped in blankets and with bandages round their heads. The darkness resounded with hollow, tubercular coughs, drowning the murmur of liturgical Latin. When mass was over, I went out into the courtyard where the flagstones were shiny with rain. Convalescent soldiers were strolling about there, their cheeks gaunt and their eyes sunken with the effects of fever. In the dawn light they looked like ghosts. They were nearly all village lads, ill with fatigue and home-sickness. Only one had been wounded in battle. I went over to talk to him. As I approached, he stood to attention and I asked him:

'How are you, lad?'

'Waiting for them to throw me out into the street.'

'Where were you wounded?'

'In the head.'

'I mean in what action.'

'A skirmish near Otáiz.'

'Which troops were involved?'

'It was just us against two companies from Ciudad Rodrigo.'

'And who is "us"?'

'We're the priest's boys. It was the first time I'd been under fire.'

'And which priest is that?'

'The one from Estella.'

'Brother Ambrosio?'

'I think so, yes.'

'Don't you know him?'

'No, sir. Our leader was Miquelcho. People said the priest was wounded.'

'You weren't in the original group then?'

'No, sir. Me and about three others joined up when they passed through Omellín.'

'And they forced you to follow them?'

'Yes, sir. They were levying troops.'

'And how did the priest's lads fight?'

'I thought we did well. We killed at least seven of the red-trousered brigade. We hid on a slope by the road. They were walking along singing, not a care in the world . . .'

The boy broke off. There was the distant clamour of frightened female voices that echoed through the house, shouting:

'This is terrible!'

'Holy Mother of God!'

'Holy Jesus!'

The clamour suddenly stopped. Silence was restored. The soldiers were talking about what had happened, and various versions of the event were given. I was walking beneath the arches and, even without paying much attention, I caught fragments that told me the bare bones of the story. In one group they spoke of an ancient, bedridden nun who had set fire to the curtains around her bed, in another group they talked of a novice found dead in her cell by the brazier. Weary of walking beneath the arches where the rain gusted in on the wind, I went to my room. In one corridor I met Sister Jimena.

'What is all the crying about, Sister?'

The nun hesitated for a moment and then replied, smiling and innocent:

'What crying?'

She knew nothing. She was busy distributing food to the boys. It was terrible to see the state the poor things were in.

I did not want to press her further and so I went back to my cell. My soul was filled with a decadent and subtle sadness, the latent lust of the mystic and the poet. The morning sun, a pale winter sun, trembled on the panes of the narrow window that looked out ohto the road lined by leafless poplars and the backdrop of sombre mountains stained with snow. Soldiers were still arriving in scattered groups. The nuns, who were gathered in the garden, received them with loving solicitude and bound their wounds after first washing them with miraculous water. I could hear the dull murmur of distressed and angry voices. They were all saying that they had been betrayed. I sensed then th˄t the war was nearing its end and, gazing out at the austere peaks from which came both eagles and betrayal, I remembered the words of the Queen:

'Bradomín, do not let it be said of the knights of Spain that you went off to distant lands in search of a princess only to dress her in mourning.'

Someone rapped on the door. I turned round and saw Sister Simona standing there. Her voice was so changed, I had not recognised it. Fixing me with imperious eyes, she said:

'I have some good news for you, Marquis.'

She paused, in order to give more weight to her words, and, staying precisely where she was, standing motionless in the doorway, she said:

'The doctor says that you can leave and be on your way, that you are out of danger.'

I looked at her, surprised, trying to divine her thoughts, but her face remained impenetrable, hidden in the shadow of her wimple. Slowly, imitating the haughty tone with which she had spoken to me, I said:

'When should I leave, Reverend Mother?'

'Whenever you wish.'

Sister Simona made as if to go and with a gesture I stopped her:

'One moment, Reverend Mother.'

'What do you want?'

'I want to say goodbye to the young girl who kept me company during these sad days.'

'The girl is ill.'

'And I can't see her?'

'No, the cells are cloistered.'

She was already half-way out of the room when, firmly retracing her steps, she came back in and closed the door. With a voice vibrant with anger and heavy with sorrow, she said:

'In making that girl fall in love with you, you have committed the most loathsome of crimes.'

I confess that her accusation only awoke in my soul a feeling of sweet, sentimental regret.

'Sister Simona, do you imagine that with my white hair and my missing arm I am still capable of making someone fall in love with me?'

The nun fixed me with eyes that flashed angrily out at me from beneath heavily lined eyelids.

'You can if the girl in question is an angel. Since you can no longer make conquests with your fine physique, you put on a manly melancholy that moves the heart to pity. Poor girl, she confessed everything to me.'

Bowing my head, I said:

'Poor girl.'

Sister Simona stepped back and shouted:

'You knew.'

I felt troubled and uneasy. A heavy black cloud wrapped about my soul and a flat, unemphatic voice, the unfamiliar voice of doom, spoke inside me like a sleepwalker. I felt the terror of all my sins upon me as if I were about to die. My past years seemed full of shadows, like pools of stagnant water. That intuitive voice inside me implacably repeated words which come back to me now with stubborn persistence. The nun clasping her hands together cried out in horror:

'You knew.'

And that voice laden with the full horror of my guilt made me tremble. I felt as if I were dead and were hearing it from inside the tomb, like an accusation from the world. The mystery of those sweet, sad, velvet eyes was the mystery of the melancholy I used to feel when I was a young man and a poet. Beloved eyes! I had loved them because I found in them the romantic sighs of my youth, the sentimental longings which, when they foundered, had made of me a cynic, the melancholy, Don Juanesque perversion that weeps along with the victims it itself creates. The nun's words, repeated again and again, seemed to fall on me like drops of molten metal:

'You knew.'

I kept a sombre silence. I examined my conscience, wanting to punish my soul with the hairshirt of remorse, but that consolation of all repentant sinners, that too eluded me. I thought that my guilt could not be compared with that of our original sin, and I even regretted, along with Jacopo Casanova, that parents cannot always make their children happy. With her hands clasped and that note of horror and doubt still in her voice, Sister Simona kept repeating:

'You knew. You knew.'

And then, suddenly, fixing me with ardent, fanatical eyes, she made the sign of the cross and began hurling curses at me. I left the room as if I were the Devil himself. I went down into the courtyard where some of the soldiers in my escort were chatting to the wounded men there, and I gave orders for the horses to be saddled up. Shortly afterwards, the bugle uttered its notes, bright and arrogant as a cockerel crowing. The ten lancers in my escort gathered together in the square. Held in check by their riders, the horses were pawing the ground outside the doorway above which stood the coat of arms. When I mounted my horse, I so felt the lack of my arm that I was filled by a sense of profound despair and, seeking the balm of those velvet eyes, I looked up at the windows, but the narrow windows glittering in the morning sun remained firmly closed. I asked for the reins to be handed to me and, sunk in bitter thought, I rode on ahead of my lancers. As we went up a hill, I turned round to send my last sigh back to that old house where I had encountered the most beautiful love of my life. On the panes of one window I saw the tremor of many reflected lights, and the presentiment of the misfortune that the nuns had sought to conceal from me fluttered over my soul like the sombre flight of a bat. I dropped the reins and covered my eyes with my hand, so that my soldiers would not see me cry. In that grim state of grief, depression and uncertainty, a few childish words tormented my fevered memory: She's dreadfully plain, plain, plain!

That was the saddest day of my life. My griefs and my thoughts gave me not a moment's peace. One minute I would be burning with fever, the next I would be shivering, my teeth chattering. Sometimes I was filled by a wild delirium, and strange, grotesque, futile ideas became transmuted into the anxious ramblings of a nightmare. When, at nightfall, we rode into the streets of Estella, I could barely keep myself in the saddle, and when I dismounted, I almost fell to the ground. I stayed in a house with two ladies – mother and daughter – the mother being the widow of the famous Don Miguel de Arizcun. I still vividly remember those two ladies dressed in their serge habits; I remember their faded faces, their thin hands, their noiseless footsteps and their nun-like voices. They attended me with loving solicitude, giving me soup and plenty of wine and constantly peering round the door of my room to see if I was asleep or if I needed anything. When night had fallen, there were great poundings at the door that echoed throughout the house, and the daughter came into my room, looking rather frightened:

'Marquis, someone wants to see you.'

A very tall man appeared at the door of my room, his head bandaged, his cape about his shoulders. In a voice as grave as if he were intoning a prayer for the dead he said:

'I greet our illustrious leader and deeply regret your misfortune.'

It was Brother Ambrosio and I could not but rejoice to see him. He came over to my bed, spurs jingling and with his right hand clutching his brow in an attempt to control the shaking of his head. As she took her leave, the lady said in mellifluous tones:

'Try not to tire him, and speak softly.'

Brother Ambrosio nodded. We were left alone and, when he had sat down at my bedside, he began mumbling various trite phrases:

'To think that after all your travels and all the dangers you have faced, you should lose an arm in this war, which is not even a real war. We can never know when misfortune will befall us, nor good fortune for that matter, and as for death . . . We know nothing. Happy the man who does not die in mortal sin when his final hour comes.'

It diverted me from my sorrows listening to that warrior-monk's words. I knew that I was supposed to find his words edifying, but I could not help but feel a wave of incipient laughter rising inside me. Seeing me pale and gaunt with fever, Brother Ambrosio had judged me to be on the point of death and he was glad to put aside for a moment his bluff soldier's guise, in order to set safely on the path to the other world the soul of a friend who was dying for the cause. He was as happy waging war against the *alfonsistas* as he was against Satan. The bandage, which he wore like a turban about his head, had slipped back slightly to reveal the bloody slit of a knife wound in his temple. Buried in the pillows, I moaned and said in a faint, mocking voice:

'Brother Ambrosio, you still haven't told me about your adventures, nor how you received that wound.'

He stood up. He looked as fierce as an ogre, indeed I found him just as diverting as the ogres in fairy tales.

'You want to know how I received this wound? As ingloriously as you did yours. Adventures? There are no adventures any more, there's no war any more, it's all an utter farce. The *alfonsista* generals flee from us and we flee from the *alfonsista* generals. This war is all about collecting promotions and new reasons to be ashamed. I tell you it will all end with a sell-out, just like the first war. There are plenty of generals in the *alfonsista* camp who would be happy to act as go-betweens. That's how you get to be a general these days!'

He fell into an ill-humoured silence, struggling to adjust his bandage. His hands and his head were both trembling. His ugly, bare cranium was reminiscent of the skull of one those giant Moors who rise up, dripping blood, beneath the horse of the Apostle. I said to him with a smile:

'I'm tempted to say, Brother Ambrosio, that I'm glad that the cause will not triumph.'

He looked at me, astonished:

'Do you mean that?'

'Absolutely.'

And it was true. I have always thought that fallen majesty was far more beautiful than the enthroned variety; indeed my reasons for defending tradition have always been purely aesthetic. For me, Carlism has all the solemn charm of great cathedrals, and even in time of war, I would gladly have had it declared a national monument. I think I can say, without boasting, that the King is of the same opinion. Brother Ambrosio opened wide his arms and unleashed the thunder of his voice.

'The reason the cause will not triumph is because there are too many traitors.'

He remained silent for a moment, frowning, clutching his bandaged head, revealing the terrible knife wound. I asked him again:

'Come on, tell me how you got that wound, Brother Ambrosio.'

He tried to set the bandage straight as he stammered:

'I don't know . . . I can't remember.'

I looked at him uncomprehendingly. Brother Ambrosio was standing by my bed and his bare, shaking skull gleamed white in the darkness. Shadows covered the wall. Suddenly, hurling what remained of the bandage to the ground, he exclaimed:

'We know each other well, Marquis, and I know that you are perfectly aware of how I got this wound, and that you are only asking in order to embarrass me.'

When I heard this, I sat up, and said with lofty disdain:

'Brother Ambrosio, I have suffered too much in these last few days to waste my time worrying about you.'

He frowned and bowed his head:

'That's true. You have had your problems too. Well, it was that thief Miquelcho who split my head open. The traitor took over command of the troops. I'll pay him back one day.

170

Believe me, the terrible things I said to you that night weigh heavy on me. But what's done is done, and fortunately, you, Marquis, are capable of understanding all things.'

I broke in:

'And of forgiving them too, Brother Ambrosio.'

His anger subsided into gloom, and, sighing, he slumped into an armchair at my bedside. After some time, while he felt around under his cape, he said:

'That's what I've always said. You're the finest gentleman in all Spain. Well, here are four gold coins for you. I don't imagine you want to check their assay value. They say that only Jews do that.'

He had taken the money, wrapped in a piece of paper stained with snuff, from the lining of his cape and his jocund laughter recalled the laughter you hear in the vast refectories of monasteries. I said to him with the sigh of a sinner:

'Keep them to pay for a mass.'

His black mouth opened in a smile:

'A mass for what?'

'For the triumph of the cause.'

He got up out of the chair, as if to bring the visit to an end. I was looking at him from where I lay on my pillows, and I kept an ironic silence, because I could see that he was hesitating. Then he said:

'I have a message from a certain lady. She wants you to know that she still loves you, but she begs you not to try and see her.'

I sat up amongst the pillows, surprised and shocked. I recalled the trap that had been laid for me by this same friar, and I judged his words to be some new trick. With proud disdain I told him so and showed him the door. He started to reply, but, without saying another word, I merely repeated the same imperious gesture. Muttering under his breath, he slammed out of the room. The noise boomed about the house, and the two ladies appeared at the door, a look of innocent alarm on their faces.

I enjoyed a refreshing, easeful sleep that night. The bells of the neighbouring church woke me at dawn and, some time afterwards, the two ladies who were looking after me appeared at the door of my room, each wearing a headscarf and with a rosary wrapped about their wrist. Their voices, gestures and dresses were identical. They greeted me in the rather unctuous fashion that devout ladies do. They smiled the same sweet, childlike smile that seemed to spread into the mystical shadows cast by their scarves which they wore fastened to their hair with long pins made out of jet.

I said quietly:

'Are you going to mass?'

'No, we've just come from there.'

'What news in Estella?'

'What do you want to know?'

Their two voices chimed together like a litany, and the half-light of the bedroom served only to increase their nun-like appearance. I decided to ask outright:

'Do you know how the Count Volfani is?'

They looked at each other, and I believe that a blush tinged their sallow cheeks. There was a moment's silence and the daughter left the room, obeying a gesture from her mother, who had watched over her daughter's prim innocence for more than forty years. At the door, she turned and smiled, the innocent, faded smile of an old maid.

'I'm so glad you're feeling better, Marquis.'

And with neat, modest steps she disappeared into the shadows of the corridor. Feigning indifference, I continued my talk with her mother:

'Volfani is like a brother to me. He had an accident the day we left and I don't know how he is.'

The woman sighed:

'Well, he has not yet fully recovered consciousness. The person I feel sorry for is the Countess. When they brought him to her, she spent five days and nights at his bedside. And now they say that she looks after him and serves him like another St Isabel.'

I confess that the almost posthumous love that María Antonieta was showing for her husband filled me with a mixture of astonishment and sadness. In the days I had spent contemplating my amputated arm and allowing myself to dream, it had often seemed to me that the blood from my wound and the tears from her eyes were falling on our sinful love and purifying it. I had felt the ideal consolation of her womanly love becoming transmuted into an exalted, mystical Franciscan love. My heart beat jealously. I said:

'And the Count has not improved?'

'He has improved, but he's like a child. They dress him and sit him in a chair and that's where he spends the day. Apparently he doesn't recognise anyone.'

The lady was removing her scarf as she spoke, folding it carefully and then sticking the pins in it. Since I said nothing more, she clearly judged that she should leave:

'I'll come and see you later, Marquis, but if you want anything, you only have to call.'

As she left, she paused in the doorway, listening to the sound of footsteps approaching. She looked out, and said:

'I'm leaving you in good company. Here's Brother Ambrosio.'

Surprised, I sat up. He entered, spluttering:

'I should never again have set foot in this house after the way you treated me, sir, but your unworthy servant Brother Ambrosio will forgive a friend anything.'

I held out my hand to him.

'Let's talk no more about it. I know of our Countess Volfani's conversion.'

'And what do you have to say? Do you understand now how ill-deserved your arrogant remarks of yesterday were? I was merely the emissary, a humble emissary.'

Brother Ambrosio squeezed my hand until my bones cracked. I said again:

'Let's talk no more about it.'

'But we must talk. Do you still doubt that I am your friend?'

It was a solemn moment and I took advantage of it to free my hand and press it to my heart:

'Never!'

He got up.

'I have seen the Countess.'

'And what does our saint have to say?'

'She says that she is prepared to see you one last time in order to say goodbye.'

When I heard that, rather than happiness, I felt a shadow of sadness cover my soul. Was it perhaps the sadness of having to show myself to her lovely eyes in this unpoetic state, and with one arm missing?

Leaning on the friar's arm, I left my lodgings to go to the King's house. A pale sun was making inroads into the leaden clouds, and the white wake of snow, lingering in the shelter of the sombre walls, was beginning to melt. I walked along in silence. With romantic sadness I evoked the history of my loves and savoured the mortuary perfume of María Antonieta's farewell. The friar told me that, out of saintly scruple, she did not wish to meet me in her own home, but would await me in the King's house. Equally scrupulous, I had declared with a sigh that the purpose of my visit to the King's house was not to see her but to pay my respects to the Queen. When I went into the anteroom I was afraid I might weep. I remembered that other day when I had kissed her pale, royal, blue-veined hand and how I had felt like a paladin eager to consecrate his life to his Queen. For the first time, I found a proud and lofty consolation for my ugly, one-armed state, that of having spilled my blood for that princess, as pale and saintly as a princess in a legend, who, surrounded by her ladies, sat embroidering scapulars for the soldiers of the cause. When I went in, some ladies stood up, as they used to do when respected members of the church entered. The Queen said to me:

'I had news of your misfortune, and I prayed long and hard for you. God chose to save your life.'

I bowed deeply:

'God chose not to allow me to die for you.'

Moved by my words, the ladies wiped the tears from their eyes. I smiled sadly, reflecting to myself that, in future, that was the attitude I would have to adopt with ladies in order to make my one-armed state seem poetic. With utter sincerity, the Queen said:

'Men like you have no need of arms, your heart is all you need.'

'Thank you, your Majesty!'

There were a few brief moments of silence, and a bishop who was present said in a low voice:

'Our Lord God has allowed you to keep your right hand, the hand you use for the pen and for the sword.'

The prelate's words provoked a murmur of admiration amongst the ladies. I turned round and my eyes met María Antonieta's. A mist of tears made them seem still brighter. I greeted her with a slight smile and she remained serious, looking at me hard. The prelate approached, priestly and benevolent:

'Our beloved Marquis must have suffered greatly.'

I nodded and His Grace half-closed his eyes in a gesture of grave compassion.

'I'm so very sorry.'

The ladies sighed. Only Doña Margarita remained silent and serene. Her princess' heart told her that, as far as my pride was concerned, pity was tantamount to humiliation. The prelate went on:

'Now that you will be forced to rest, you should write a book about your life.'

The Queen said, smiling:

'Yes, Bradomín, your memoirs would make most interesting reading.'

And the Marchioness of Tor grunted:

'He'd be sure to leave out the really interesting bits.'

I replied, bowing:

'I would mention only my sins.'

The Marchioness of Tor, my aunt and a great lady, made some other mumbled comment that I did not quite catch. The prelate continued in his sermonising tones:

'I've heard some extraordinary things about our illustrious Marquis. Confessions, when they are sincere, are always of great educational value. One has only to think of St Augustine. Of course, pride often blinds us and one can make of such books a mere vulgar display of sins and vices. Consider only that impious philosopher from Geneva. In such cases the bright lesson that one normally gleans from confessions, the crystalline spring water of doctrine, grows muddy.'

Bored with the sermon, the ladies were talking in low voices. Seated some way off, María Antonieta appeared absorbed in her work and was saying nothing. The edifying effect of the prelate's talk seemed to be aimed only at me, and, since I am not a selfish man, I decided to sacrifice myself for the ladies, and humbly interrupted him:

'I do not aspire to teach, but to amuse. My whole doctrine lies in a single phrase: Hurrah for bagatelles! For me, human-kind's greatest triumph is having learned how to smile.'

There was a ripple of delighted, frivolous laughter, which made one doubt for a moment that men could have been totally serious for long centuries at a time and that whole ages could have passed during which History records not a single famous smile.

His Grace raised his arms to Heaven:

'It is likely, nay almost certain, that the ancients never said "Hurrah for bagatelles!", like our frenchified Marquis here. Only do your best, Marquis, not to be damned for a mere bagatelle. I'm sure people have always smiled in Hell.'

I was about to respond, but the Queen was eyeing me sternly. With learned solemnity, the prelate gathered his habits about him and, adopting that aggressive but affable tone favoured by theologians engaging in debates in the seminary, he launched into a long sermon.

With the familiar, surly manner that all my devout, old aunts adopted when addressing me, the Marchioness of Tor called me over to the balcony. I went reluctantly, knowing that she would have nothing pleasant to say to me. Her first words confirmed my fears.

'I didn't expect to see you here. I assume you'll be leaving shortly.'

In a slightly sentimental tone, I said:

'I would like to obey you, but my heart prevents my leaving.'

'It's not me telling you to leave, it's that poor creature.'

And with a glance she indicated María Antonieta. I sighed, covering my eyes with my hand.

'And does that same poor creature refuse to say goodbye to me, even though it is for ever?'

My noble aunt hesitated. Despite her wrinkles and her severe expression, she retained the sentimental candour of old ladies who, as young women, had attended literary gatherings.

'Xavier, don't try to take her away from her husband. You, better than anyone, must understand what a sacrifice that is for her. She wants to remain faithful to that shadow dragged back by some miracle from the very brink of death.'

She spoke in an emotional and dramatic manner, clutching my hand in her withered hands. I said in a low voice, fearful that I might not be able to speak for emotion.

'What harm can it do for us to say goodbye? She was the one who wanted it.'

'Because you demanded it, and the poor woman did not have the courage to refuse you. María Antonieta wants to live for ever in your heart. She wants to give you up, but not your affection. I am very old and I know the world and I know you intend to commit some folly. Xavier, if you cannot respect her sacrifice, at least try not to make it even more cruel.'

178

The Marchioness wiped away a tear. I said with melancholy resentment:

'So you think I won't respect her sacrifice! You're unfair to me, but, in that, you're being true to family tradition. It grieves me so, the idea that you all have of me. God, who can read in all our hearts . . .'

My aunt recovered her imperious tone:

'Be quiet. You are the most admirable of all Don Juans, ugly, Catholic and sentimental.'

She was so old, the good lady, that she had forgotten the fickleness of the female heart and the fact that when a man is missing one arm and his hair is nearly white, he must give up any pretensions to being a Don Juan. Ah, I knew that the sad, velvet eyes that had opened to me like two Franciscan flowers in the dawn light would be the last to look on me with love. Now the only possible attitude for me to take towards women was that of a cold, broken, indifferent idol. Realising all this for the first time, I gave a sad smile and showed the old lady the empty sleeve of my uniform. Then, moved by the memory of the young girl shut up in that old house, I had to lie a little when speaking of María Antonieta.

'María Antonieta is the only woman who still loves me. Her love is all that's left to me in the world. I was resigned to never seeing her again and, filled with disillusion, I was just considering becoming a friar when I learned that she wanted to say goodbye to me for the last time . . .'

'And what if I asked you to leave now?'

'You?'

'On behalf of María Antonieta.'

'I think I deserve to hear that from her.'

'And does the poor woman not deserve to be spared that new pain?'

'Even if I do as you say today, she may call me back tomorrow. Do you imagine that the Christian piety that now draws her to her husband will last for ever?'

Before she could respond, I heard a tearful voice behind me say:

'Yes, Xavier, for ever.'

I turned round and found myself face to face with María Antonieta. She was standing utterly still and looking at me with eyes ablaze. I showed her my amputated arm and, with a look of horror, she closed her eyes. She seemed to have aged greatly. María Antonieta was very tall and full of a proud majesty, her black hair now streaked with white. She had the mouth of a statue and her cheeks were like withered flowers, the cheeks of a penitent – gaunt and aloof – that seemed to live bereft of kisses and caresses. Her eyes were dark and febrile, her voice grave, like molten metal. There was something strange about her, as if she could hear the flutter of departing souls and could communicate with them at the midnight hour. After a long, painful silence, she said again.

'Yes, Xavier, for ever.'

I looked at her hard.

'Longer than my love for you?'

'For as long as your love lasts.'

The Marchioness, who was glancing myopically about the room, said in a quiet, advisory voice:

'If you must talk, then do it somewhere else.'

María Antonieta nodded and moved off, her face set, saying nothing, just as some of the other ladies were beginning to give us curious looks. At almost the same moment, two of the King's dogs burst into the room. Don Carlos followed moments later. When he saw me, he came over and, without uttering a single word, gave me a long embrace. Then he began talking to me in the slightly joking tone he always adopted, as if nothing about me had changed. I confess that no other demonstration of his affection for me could have moved me as much as that generous display of delicacy.

My aunt indicated to me that I should follow her and led me to her room where María Antonieta was waiting for me, weeping and alone. When she saw me come in, she stood up, fixing me with reddened, shining eyes. She was breathing hard and she spoke in a tense, hoarse voice:

'Xavier, we must say goodbye. You have no idea how I have suffered since that night we parted.'

I interrupted her and said, with a vague, sentimental smile:

'Do you remember that we parted promising to love each other always?'

It was her turn to interrupt me.

'You have come here to ask me to abandon a poor sick man and I can never, never do that. That would be dishonourable.'

'Love sometimes demands that we act dishonourably, but, alas, I am now too old for any woman to do so for me.'

'Xavier, I have to sacrifice myself.'

'A rather belated sacrifice, María Antonieta.'

'You're very cruel.'

'Cruel!'

'You mean that my sacrifice should have been not to neglect my duties.'

'That might have been better, but if I blame you, I have to blame myself too. Neither of us was capable of sacrificing ourselves, because that is a science that one only learns with the years, when one's heart finally freezes over.'

'Xavier, this is the last time that we will see each other, and your words will leave me with such bitter memories.'

'Do you really think this is the last time? I don't. If I did give in to your pleas, you would only call me back again.'

'Why do you say that? Even if I were such a coward as to call you back, you wouldn't come. Our love is impossible now.'

'I would always come back.'

181

María Antonieta raised her eyes to heaven, eyes made lovelier by tears, and she murmured as if in prayer:

'Oh God, perhaps one day my resolve will falter and my cross become too much for me . . .'

I went over to her and stood so close I could feel her breath. I took her hands in mine.

'That day has come.'

'Never, never!'

She tried to pull away from me, but couldn't. I whispered, almost in her ear:

'Aren't you sure? That day is here.'

'Go, Xavier! Leave me!'

'How you wound me with your scruples, María Antonieta.'

'Go, go! Don't say anything more. I don't want to hear you.'

I kissed her hands.

'The divine scruples of a saint.'

'Be quiet!'

With frightened eyes, she moved away from me. There was a long silence. María Antonieta drew her hands across her brow and breathed deeply. Gradually she grew calmer. There was a light of desperate resolution in her eyes when she said:

'Xavier, I am going to have to hurt you badly now. I wanted you to love me as if I were a bride of fifteen. I must have been mad. I have not told you the truth about myself.'

'I don't mind.'

'I've had other lovers.'

'Well, that's life.'

'You don't despise me?'

'I can't.'

'But you're smiling.'

I said calmly:

'My poor María Antonieta, I am smiling because I can find no reason to be harsh with you. Some men want to be a woman's first lover, but I have always preferred to be their last. Ah, but will I be?'

'Such cruel words!'

'Life is cruel, unless we are prepared to walk through it like blind children.'

'You do despise me. That is my penance.'

'No, I don't despise you. You used to be just like all women, no better, no worse. Now you're going to be a saint. Goodbye, María Antonieta.'

María Antonieta was sobbing, tearing at her lace handkerchief with her teeth. She slumped down on the sofa. I remained standing close by her. There was a silence full of sighs. María Antonieta dried her eyes, looked at me and smiled sadly.

'Xavier, if all women are as you judge me to be, then perhaps I have not been quite the same as them. Pity me then, but bear me no malice.'

'It isn't malice that I feel, it's the melancholy of disillusion, a melancholy that feels as if the winter snow had fallen on my soul, as if my soul, like a wasteland, had made of it a shroud.'

'You'll know the love of other women.'

'I fear they might notice that my hair has turned white and that I have one arm missing.'

'What does your missing arm matter, or your white hair! I would seek them out in order to love them all the more. Goodbye, Xavier . . . for ever.'

'Who knows what life may have in store for us? Goodbye, María Antonieta.'

Those were our last words. Then she silently held out her hand to me, I kissed it and we parted. As I went out of the door, I was tempted to turn around, but I resisted. War may not have given me the opportunity to show my heroism, but love did as it bade me farewell, perhaps for ever.

AFTERWORD

Valle-Inclán was born in Galicia in 1866 and died there in 1936. He spent most of his adult life in Madrid writing newspaper articles, short stories, novels and plays, and participating vociferously in the literary circles that met in many of the cafés. Like Bradomín he was (at least for a time) a Carlist, or claimed to be. However, with typical unpredictability, he later espoused republicanism, later still, became a self-styled anarchist and, on his deathbed, adamantly refused the last rites.

He wrote the *Sonatas* in the 'wrong' order, starting with *Autumn* in 1902 and followed by *Summer* (1903), *Spring* (1904) and *Winter* (1905). They are now always published following the usual cycle of the seasons, since each *Sonata* shows the narrator, the Marquis of Bradomín, at an appropriate stage in his life.

Valle-Inclán once described Bradomín as 'an admirable Don Juan, perhaps the most admirable.' Bradomín was, he said, 'ugly, Catholic and sentimental', a description that Valle-Inclán also applied to himself, for the character shares much of his creator's personality – by turns self-important and self-mocking. This aspect of the narrator of the *Sonatas* is part and parcel of the book's intensely self-conscious style. Valle-Inclán's Don Juan knows about other Don Juans – literary and real-life; and he is writing these memoirs in a style that plagiarises, parodies and celebrates the style of such literary (and Catholic) libertines as D'Annunzio, Barbey D'Aurevilly, Huysmans, etc. There is, in short, something inescapably mannered, one might say 'camp', about the *Sonatas*.

Valle-Inclán wove endless myths around his own life, regaling his café companions, for example, with wildly exaggerated stories about his year in Mexico, about duels never actually fought. He also recycled his real experiences in his fiction. The amputation of Bradomín's arm in *Winter Sonata* is a glorified version of the operation Valle-Inclán underwent after a wound – inflicted on him by a friend with a walking stick during a foolish argument – became gangrenous. Like his hero, Valle-Inclán had the operation without any anaesthetic, by choice – he wanted to see for himself what happened. However, whereas Bradomín endures the whole operation without so much as a murmur, Valle-Inclán, being human, fainted half-way through. (He did not, as far as I know, use another incident when he literally shot himself in the foot whilst prospecting for mercury ore!) Equally, Valle-Inclán often retold episodes from his fiction as if they were episodes from his own life. Like his hero, Bradomín, he was always remodelling and idealizing his past.

The character of Bradomín had already appeared in some of Valle-Inclán's earlier fictions and, long after the *Sonatas* were written, he resurfaced towards the end of Valle-Inclán's play *Luces de Bohemia* (*Bohemian Lights*) as a near-centenarian. Bradomín was one of Valle-Inclán's alter egos in that he was the kind of man Valle-Inclán might have liked to be at a particular time of his life. Creator and character share a liking for the theatrical. Any Don Juan is, by definition, an exhibitionist and Bradomín is no exception; he enjoys being the centre of attention, and is not surprised when he is urged to write his memoirs or when the priests listen avidly to his (invented) tales. He is theatrical in appearance as well – he wears an extravagant, outmoded zouave uniform and, at one point, disguises himself as a monk. Valle-Inclán too turned himself into a spectacle. He constantly reinvented himself – Carlist, bohemian, dandy, journalist, family man, actor, republican, anarchist. He grew his beard and hair long from the age of seventeen, adopted various striking outfits – long capes, strange hats, rimless glasses, horn-rimmed glasses, white spats – always slightly out of kilter with the current fashions, and was probably one of the most photographed and painted of Spanish writers. After his arm was amputated, and having experimented briefly with an artificial limb, he left the sleeve of his jacket ostentatiously empty; he became an iconic figure in his own lifetime. For all these reasons, it is often difficult to disentangle creator from character.

In Valle-Inclán's version, the Don Juan myth of irrepressible potency is progressively undercut as we follow Bradomín's progress from young blade to middle-aged companion to silver-haired seducer anxious about his failing sexual powers. Sexual myths or icons should not grow old – it is difficult to imagine Marilyn Monroe, for example, at sixty or seventy. Unlike most other Don Juans, Bradomín is not punished with Hell, even though he has been as sacrilegious and libidinous as any. Bradomín's punishment, if indeed Valle-Inclán intended it as one, is the dread knowledge, at the end of *Winter Sonata*, that love may have bade farewell to him for ever.

Equally atypical is the fact that we are vouchsafed glimpses of Bradomín as a child – most Don Juans seem never to have had a childhood. He is described as a little boy being read to by his aunt, or jumping up and down with his cousins in order to make the ornaments on the sideboard tremble. Perhaps more psychologically telling to the reader – given Bradomín's later career as a Don Juan – is his remark to Concha that his first conquest was his Aunt Augusta, who fell in love with him when he was only eleven.

This is not to say that Bradomín does not share certain Don Juan characteristics, but these always have an unconventional edge. Bradomín is certainly a womaniser, but on two occasions he regrets – as if it were some personal failing – that he has never enjoyed the love of other men. He has had many conquests, but he is not coarsely concerned with keeping a tally of his successes. While some of his ex-lovers do fear and hate him – Rosario and her mother in *Spring Sonata,* for example, abhor his apparently diabolical nature – others remain genuinely fond of him – Concha in *Autumn Sonata* and the Duchess of Uclés in *Winter Sonata.* Like most Don Juans, Bradomín suffers little guilt at the havoc he blithely causes in women's hearts and lives; but he is troubled (however fleetingly) by the thought that he is, on occasion, hated, and he seems genuinely unnerved, nonplussed even, that his name should be so repeatedly linked with that of the Devil. For a Don Juan, Bradomín is unusually concerned with appearances. He sometimes seduces a woman out of pure politeness – his cousin Isabel and María Antonieta – so that they are not humiliated by the real, unflattering reason for his presence in their bedroom or their home. What most marks him out from other Don Juans is his attitude to love. Bradomín is, of course, a great sensualist and there are some remarkably frank and erotic scenes in the books, but, unlike many Don Juans, he likes to give pleasure to women, and indeed openly distrusts those women who preoccupy themselves with pleasuring their men. He gives love and pleasure in order to receive love and admiration back. Sexual conquest is not enough for Bradomín – he needs to be loved. After Concha's death, he does not mourn *her*, but the fact that no one will ever love him as absolutely as she did. His fear in *Winter Sonata* – and what drives him on in his seduction of the innocent Maximina – is that no woman will ever look on him with love again.

Bradomín is also a Romantic Don Juan, for sex, religion and death – those favourite Romantic themes – are an inextricable part of the fabric of the *Sonatas*. Valle-Inclán characteristically mixes religious and sexual language and mingles sex and death. For example, in *Autumn Sonata*, Bradomín is sexually aroused by Concha's guilt-ridden piety, her physical frailty and his own terror at her nearness to death. When Concha actually dies in mid-embrace, her prayers to the Virgin to let her die with Bradomín by her side are perversely, not to say grotesquely, answered. Bradomín likes his women to be pious, he likes them to surrender themselves to him despite all their religious principles. That, for him, heightens the sexual excitement of the moment. Again, all this is done very knowingly by the author. Valle-Inclán is aware that he is using well-worn Romantic themes; the trick is to ride that fine line between taking them utterly seriously and mocking their creaking pretentiousness.

In his recent book (*Valle-Inclán: Los botines blancos de piqué*,

190

1998), Francisco Umbral argues that the model for Bradomín is not so much Casanova as the Marquis de Sade. However, in *Autumn Sonata*, Bradomín explicitly denies any such judgement. There is, I think, some basis for describing Bradomín as a sadist, and there is undoubtedly a masochistic streak in most of the women he encounters; I still feel, however, that Bradomín, like all Don Juans, is chiefly a narcissist, and that his cruelty is just another aspect of his narcissism rather than of overt sadism. Any acts of cruelty he commits are more casual than premeditated and are often laced with kindness. For example, his seduction of Concha in *Autumn Sonata* despite her religious qualms and her precarious health, is not only to satisfy his own desires, but Concha's too. He makes Concha happy. He may be cruel, but he can also be oddly considerate.

Essentially, Bradomín loves only himself and cares only about the kind of figure he cuts in the world. His first thought after his left arm is amputated is 'what attitude should I adopt from then on, when in the company of women, in order to make the loss of my arm seem poetic'. He forgets that the Duchess of Uclés has borne him a child; then, once he has assured himself that the Duchess is not lying, his reaction is a selfish one: 'I suddenly sensed the love of that distant, almost illusory daughter.' Perhaps the most extreme and disturbing example of his narcissism, though, is his seduction of Maximina, despite the nagging inner voice that keeps telling him that she may well be his daughter. He makes her fall in love with him simply in order to prove to himself that, even with only one arm, he is still the great seducer. He is not concerned with what consequences this might have for Maximina, and he leaves the hospital without even bothering to find out exactly what has happened to her. Has she killed herself? We never know. Bradomín would rather skate on the surface of things, not sully himself or his image of himself with the embarrassment of other people's pain.

Appearance, then, is more important than truth. The memoirist is, after all, interested in presenting a particular self-image to the world; experiences are transformed into a pose, a stance. This fascination with surface suffuses all four *Sonatas*. Bradomín loves women for their beauty, religion for its ritual, its colourful vestments, its altars, and he loves Carlism for its sham magnificence – the Carlists will never win the war being waged in *Winter Sonata*; for him, fallen majesty is far more beautiful than the enthroned variety.

The four novels are filled with a love of surface beauty. Valle-Inclán uses the language of the decadents to celebrate the gentle greens of northern Italy, the glittering exoticism of Mexico, the soft, drenching rain of Galicia and the icy winter winds of Navarre. Valle-Inclán is sparing with metaphors and lavish with adjectives, relying heavily on the musicality of his language to convey sense and atmosphere. Indeed, so evocative is the prose that, after a first reading of the *Sonatas*, it is often as much their atmosphere as the narrative events that remain in one's mind.

*   *   *   *

Carlism had its beginnings in the 1820s in a clerical conservative party – the a*postólicos* – which was opposed to liberalism and went on to create its own paramilitary organisation, the Royalist Volunteers. This movement gained both a sharper focus and the name 'Carlism' when Ferdinand VII's younger brother, Carlos, failed to accede to the throne on his brother's death, Ferdinand having proclaimed his daughter, Isabel, his heir. In 1833, Carlos instigated a war to claim the throne. This particularly savage war lasted for six years and ended in a compromise. One of the main conditions of the peace agreement was that Isabel would marry the son of the Pretender. When, in 1848, Isabel married someone else, there was a brief and unsuccessful second Carlist War. After an abortive coup d'état in 1860, another war ensued following the deposition of Isabel II in 1868. It is this third and last war (1870–76), that provides the setting for *Winter Sonata*. The Carlists were again defeated and the movement went into relative decline following the installation of Isabel II's son, Alfonso XII, in 1874 as a constitutional monarch. The Carlists still had some minor political force in Valle-Inclán's day, attracting those who distrusted constitutionalism and secularism and hankered after the old values of the Church and autocracy. They also held some appeal for regionalists in Galicia, Asturias, the Basque Country and Catalonia who resented the erosion of their former autonomy by an increasingly centralised government in Madrid. It seems likely that, as a Galician outsider living in Madrid, Valle-Inclán would have favoured any faction that set itself against the State and central government. At the time when he was writing the *Sonatas*, Carlism was enjoying something of a revival in the wake of Spain's humiliating defeat in the Spanish-American War of 1898 and the loss of its last remaining colony in the New World.

In *Winter Sonata*, Valle-Inclán seems to be as deeply ambivalent about the Carlist cause and Don Carlos as he is about Bradomín. He chooses as the backdrop to this final *Sonata* not the first war with its brilliant generals, but the last, disastrous Carlist War, and the novel is full of talk of betrayal, disillusionment, futility. The lofty descriptions of Don Carlos and his noble Queen are undercut by the episodes detailing the King's philandering and Volfani's stroke. Bradomín's eulogy to rape and pillage – war should be war – is as hollow as the poses he adopts in order to impress the all too impressionable Maximina. We are left with the overriding impression of a cause with a past and no future, just as Bradomín has only his past to console him.

Valle-Inclán wrote the *Sonatas* partly because he felt a genuine affection for the works of decadent writers such as Barbey d'Aurevilly and D'Annunzio, but also as a reaction against what he perceived as the banal materialism of the nineteenth-century Spanish realist novelist Benito Pérez Galdós. The *Sonatas* sold extraordinarily well when they were first published, possibly because of their rather risqué nature. Many critics of the time, though, accused Valle-Inclán of being a mere stylist. The novels *are* eminently readable, risqué and concerned with style. However, the novels are also mined with enough grotesque or absurd incidents to warn the reader to tread carefully and not to take the narratives totally at face value. A closer reading reveals the strange ambivalence I have mentioned before, the unsettling sense of a work straddling two worlds – of nineteenth-century Romantic idealism and twentieth-century ambiguity.

Margaret Jull Costa